THE WATER BEARS

THE
WATER
BEARS

KIM BAKER

WENDY
LAMB
BOOKS

Text copyright © 2020 by Kim Baker
Jacket art copyright © 2020 by Luisa Uribe

All rights reserved. Published in the United States by Wendy Lamb Books, an imprint of Random House Children's Books, a division of Penguin Random House LLC, New York.

Wendy Lamb Books and the colophon are trademarks of Penguin Random House LLC.

Visit us on the Web! rhcbooks.com

Educators and librarians, for a variety of teaching tools, visit us at RHTeachersLibrarians.com

Library of Congress Cataloging-in-Publication Data is available upon request.
ISBN 978-1-9848-5220-5 (trade)—ISBN 978-1-9848-5221-2 (lib. bdg.)—
ISBN 978-1-9848-5222-9 (ebook)

The text of this book is set in 12-point Life BT.
Interior design by Ken Crossland

Printed in the United States of America
10 9 8 7 6 5 4 3 2 1
First Edition

Random House Children's Books supports the First Amendment and celebrates the right to read.

for Sam

CHAPTER 1

I turned thirteen the day after a storm came in with a king tide.

High tides climb up part of the shore, but a king tide can make the whole beach disappear. It squeezed Murphy Island until seawater rose and salted the trees. The smell of waves pushed through the woods, through the cracks around my bedroom window, and washed away the dregs of a bad dream.

People notice details when they hope a day might be special. It could be a surprise-visitor day, a hey-I'm-starting-to-grow-a-mustache day, or a blow-out-the-candles-on-your-favorite-cake day.

I found my mom on the computer in my brother Carlos's old room. I stood in the doorway behind the desk, where she couldn't see my leg. I am an expert at keeping furniture between us, especially when it's hot enough for shorts. Even with the desk and me standing with my good leg in front of the bad one, Mom was careful not to look down. She hugged me and sang "Happy Birthday" like an opera singer. I clapped for the effort.

"Where are Dad and Little Leti?" I asked. I thought they might be out getting me a present. My sister always waits until the last minute. Or they'd gone to the bakery to pick up a cake. Dad used to make our favorites at home, but he's working more this year.

"They're down at Gertrude Lake. Everyone's down there," she said. Everyone but us. She brushed dog hair off the keyboard and straightened a stack of bills. "Your dad saw it this morning."

"Saw what?" The first thing I thought of couldn't be right, but she said it anyway.

"He saw Marvelo." She smiled again, like that was good news, or a joke, or the start of a conversation. She stretched and turned back to the computer, scrolling through recipes and fishing reports.

There was nothing to say back.

Marvelo is a creature that supposedly lives in Gertrude Lake, in the middle of the island. Optimistic tourists rent paddleboats and pump quarters into the telescopes on the beach, hoping to see it. There's a warning at the paddleboat stand that boaters might get eaten. It's a joke with the locals. Every year, Marvelo is "spotted" before the Marvelo Festival. Bits in blurry pictures could be a lake monster if you squint, or they could be logs. We have a lot of logs.

I walked slowly over the squishy mud so my leg wouldn't be too sore on the way back home. I almost stepped on a salamander, but I shooed him off the path into the ferns.

Islands are shaped like things, the way clouds are shaped like things. On a map, Murphy looks like a wonky avocado half, thirty-seven miles from the mainland. Rocky beaches and smooth mudflats are the skin, and Gertrude Lake is the pit. Everything else is the creamy green stuff that goes brown if you leave it out.

Dad stood with the pack of friends he calls comrades beside a gazebo that Mom helped build out of old farm equipment and blue bottles. The bottles hummed from a lake breeze, and Dad waved his arms toward the water.

"Just forty feet that way!" he said. "It spy-hopped and breached like a humpback, but leaner and more serpent-like. It splashed down hard enough to slosh a wake up onto the shore." Dad pointed to his still-wet shoes. The guys around him nodded, and a waiter came out from the café across the street to sell coffee and pastries to everyone standing around.

"Hey, buddy. Ready for summer?" Tom-with-the-beard tilted his head and smiled at me. He runs the paddleboat stand, and he's not my buddy. He asked how physical therapy was going, like he should get points for knowing about it. I said I was done, and he said I was brave and squeezed my shoulder, which is the absolute worst.

I shrugged and he left to rent a paddleboat to a tourist. Somebody could ride a blue cat boat or a purple fox boat out to look for Marvelo. Tom-with-the-beard must have left the paddleboats unchained, because a couple of them drifted around the lake like lost pets. Little Leti sat in the orange zebra boat still chained to the dock. She threw a basketball up and caught it, over and over.

"Newt! Come here!" Dad pulled me in for a hug. "Happy birthday, mijo! Thirteen! You feel different?" I shook my head. "Can you believe it?" I didn't know if he was talking about turning thirteen or Marvelo. My answers would have been yes and no, but he didn't wait. He spun around when someone asked about the reward. A cryptozoology club in Portland offered three thousand dollars a while back to anyone who could prove that Marvelo lived in the lake. The lake isn't huge. It's a pretty safe bet that the club will never have to write that check, no matter what Dad says. The club has reward offers for Sasquatch and jackalopes too. It's that kind of operation.

I don't even want to get into it, but my dad is writing a graphic novel about an island with two monsters called Marvelo and Manxadon. Manxadon is the sidekick, a superhero mutant that's half mastodon and half Manx cat. He stays on land, and Marvelo stays in the water. I used to help Dad sometimes, bounce around story ideas, but it's been a while. They've put short sections of the story in the Murphy newspaper a few times. People who don't think too hard about the logic love it. He wants to make it a full graphic novel, but he's too busy building condos on the mainland to ever finish.

"Is this for the book?" I said.

"Absolutely. Marvelo moved like I thought he might, but I got the skin texture totally wrong. How are you feeling, mijo?" He brushed my bangs back, but I pushed his hand away.

"Fine. Did you get any proof?"

"It's all here." He pointed to his temple.

"You need proof for the reward," I said. Dad waggled his eyebrows and rubbed his fingers together. He made it all up. If he can convince other people he saw it, then he can collect the reward. Maybe you can't blame a guy who works all the time. But maybe you can.

"I don't have proof. Yet," he said. "It's lucky I didn't pick up your present, or I would have missed Marvelo! Meet me at the ferry dock after school on Monday, and I'll give you your present then. Today I'm helping with storm cleanup. It washed Tom's patio table away!"

I nodded and waded around in the shallows, away from the crowd, so people would stop looking at my leg. Even when they think they're being subtle, I can feel it. I should have worn pants.

The water stayed flat as Dad described Marvelo all over again to a new group of passing comrades. I'm not a comrade, so I walked home.

Last year, I said I didn't care what I got for my birthday and got shirts and a sleeping bag. This year, when they asked, I said I wanted a bike. I left windows open on the computer to new bikes I liked. I ordered bike catalogs and left them lying around. No surprise camping gear this year, even if I do use the sleeping bag to sleep in the tub sometimes. Plus, the doctor said riding a bike would be good for my ligaments.

There are a finite number of bikes already on Murphy Island. None are new. A lot of them are cruisers that were here for guests to use back when the island was a fancy resort. They are older than my parents. I detoured to the bike rack near the parking lot to see if maybe Dad was just being sly and was setting me up for a surprise. A new bike would stand out like a jewel, but old island bikes filled the rack. One had a motorcycle windshield welded on and a Jolly Roger flag. The next bike had antlers for handlebars, and the one beside that was covered in Astroturf, with a raccoon tail attached to the back of the banana seat. I walked home under the whirligigs and mobiles on the pedestrians-only trail.

Mom sat on the porch with our dog, Chuck. He is a giant rescue mutt who guards our goats, unless one of us is outside, and then I guess he figures we'll do it. Chickens pecked around in the wet yard, hoping worms had come up to dry off. The grass smelled bruised from the storm and stained my wet shoes green.

"Mail came," Mom said. She handed me birthday cards from her side of the family.

"How'd it go?" She leaned out of the swing she made from old skis that sat on our porch, and balanced a row of peanuts on the railing. The phone rang inside, but she pretended not to hear it, like she usually does.

"He said he'd give me a present on Monday," I said. I sniffed. "Is that a cake?" It smelled like pineapple and banana. I opened a card from my uncle and five bucks fell out.

"Yeah. I mean by the lake. Did anyone get a picture?" Two crows flew down from the cottonwood tree to the railing on the far side of Chuck. He watched them crab-walk over to snatch the peanuts in their talons like Mom trained them to do, but he didn't move. The crows will take anything edible, whether it's meant for them or not. Sometimes they bring her buttons and lures and other shiny things they find around Murphy. She says it's a trade for the treats.

Mom and Dad asked all week if I wanted any hints about my present. They said I could never guess what it was, so I didn't. We all knew it would be a bike.

I told her that Dad and his comrades planned to take turns keeping watch at Gertrude Lake. She nodded, like watching for a lake monster was a normal way to spend a day.

"Why didn't you stay?" she asked.

I shrugged. *Because it doesn't exist,* I wanted to say. *Because it's my birthday and I hoped we would do something fun.* I crossed my fingers that he would be back in time for cake. I could blow out candles and wish to be far away on the mainland, where there are no made-up lake monsters.

CHAPTER 2

The morning after my birthday, Carlos picked me up from the ferry dock in Lincoln.

"You by yourself?" he asked.

"Mom got called in to work, so they'll meet us at abuela's house before the party," I said. Carlos nodded and offered to stop for birthday donuts.

"What's new?" Carlos asked as I opened the door to the bakery.

"My friend Rocket's cat had kittens under their porch," I said. "Two are calico boys, which he says is really rare." Carlos looked it up on his phone, and we found out that only one in three thousand calico cats is male, because of something about chromosomes.

We waited in line behind a mom letting a toddler pick his own donut. The toddler couldn't deal with having so many choices. He paced and whined, finally pointing to an orange-sprinkle one. When the clerk asked if that was his pick, he shook his head no.

"Are you guys doing an end-of-sixth-grade project?" Carlos asked.

"Yeah. A new Murphy Island brochure for the visitor center," I said.

"That's not bad. We had island-history reenactments when I was in sixth grade. Remember? I dressed up like Truman Murphy. What's your topic?" Carlos said. The toddler finally picked a chocolate cruller.

"I was thinking tide pools. Remember when Dad would take us fishing and I'd spend the whole time on the beach looking at the tide pools?" I loved lying on my stomach watching little crabs and baby octopuses. It was like an aquarium puddle.

It was our turn to order. I got an apple fritter. One obviously had more apple chunks than the others, but I didn't want to be picky like the toddler, so I didn't ask for it. The clerk grabbed the closest one, but it was small and squished looking. I wished I had said something. Carlos got a maple bar and coffee. I tried to order coffee too, but he made me get milk.

"So"—Carlos cleaned crumbs off the table—"how'd it go with Dr. Wu? He really helped my buddy Ray." He put about a million sugars into his coffee.

I picked icing off my fritter and didn't answer right away. Dr. Wu was a special kind of doctor who helped people with bad dreams after traumatic events. Insurance didn't cover my appointment, and my parents paid for it, so if it didn't help, it would be a big waste.

"It was hard to talk to a stranger, so I didn't tell him everything."

"You think it would be easier to talk to someone you know?" Carlos watched me and sipped his coffee.

"No, not really. I don't know."

"Tell me. I didn't ask before because I didn't want to stir it up for you, but maybe it would help?" He sat up and waited.

"It's not going to help," I said.

"Let's try anyway. You have somewhere to be?" He smiled.

I looked around. The toddler knocked his perfect cruller off the table and howled. His mom cleaned it up with a handful of napkins and carried him out.

"Give it a shot. Please," Carlos said.

We were alone in the store. The clerk went to the kitchen, probably praying the toddler wouldn't come back. I could feel my whole body shaking, like the shop was rumbling around me. Carlos looked so serious. "Tell me when the dreams started."

"Last year, right after it happened." He nodded. I took a bite of the fritter so he wouldn't see how close I was to crying, but it was hard to swallow. "We were at Gilda's house. You know, Mom's friend? They were inside sorting out the lineup for the festival, and I was waiting for Ethan to come rehearse our act." Ethan is my best friend. Carlos knew this part already, but I needed to work up to the other stuff.

Blackberry brambles grow all over the island. Big thorny vines popped straight out of the ground behind Gilda's house like bad luck, but the berries were delicious. "I was scared of getting poked by the thorns. Dumb, huh? I looked for berries on the creek side of the bramble, and there it was. Just like that." I tried to take deep breaths, but they just made my heart beat harder.

"A black bear, between you and the bush," Carlos said.

"My brain told me it was a big dog. The bear stood up, and I realized what it was. I tried to back up, but my feet got tangled in vines and I fell. I yelled and the bear must have felt threatened." That's what people said afterward. He got scared too. "It growled and came at me. I put my arms up over my face and tried to scoot away. It lunged, stomped on me, and bit my knee."

Carlos didn't say anything, even though it took a while for me to keep going.

"It felt like I was split in two. It took another swipe, and I screamed. Mom and Gilda heard me and ran out of the house. Mom banged a frying pan and roared. Remember how she had a scratchy voice after?" Carlos nodded. I told him how the bear took off toward the trees. It was all over in less than a minute. My leg burned like fire. I couldn't walk. I crawled through those awful vines sideways, like a crab, dragging my bloody leg through the dirt until Mom stopped me.

I didn't tell him how my skin flapped around through the rip in my jeans. Blackberry juice, dead leaves, and dirt covered the rest of me. My hands got ripped up by the bramble thorns. I hate blackberries now.

Mom and Gilda thought it was a dog at first too, when they saw what was happening from the house. There aren't usually bears on the island, but stray dogs are pretty common. We rode a floatplane to Lincoln. It was just Mom and Dad, the nurse, the pilot, and me. The ferry did a special trip to bring everyone else. People squeezed into my room until they made everybody but my parents go to the waiting room. Leti stayed at tía Birdy's house. I was all patched up by the time Carlos got to the hospital. Animal Control said the bear must have swum over from the mainland. One old woman saw it in her yard on Murphy the next day, but it disappeared after that. There were warning flyers everywhere. People stopped walking alone and even went in pairs to take their garbage out. They searched the whole island. It must have swum back to the mountains, they said.

I left a bunch out that I didn't want to talk about, but Carlos still said I remembered a lot of details. I nodded and counted fritter crumbs until my throat loosened up. My leg burned, like I needed a reminder, which I didn't. Bad memories stain everything.

"Is that what happens in the dream?" Carlos said.

"I'm mostly walking around the bramble and getting attacked." My voice cracked. The whole thing is sharp and clear. The door jingled and new customers came into the store. I didn't want them to hear me crying. "It always ends there. I don't even get to see the bear run away. But I feel the thorns and teeth and smell dirt. And bear." Bears smell awful. Dad says I dream because it's my brain's way of working it out, but not ever getting to see the bear leave feels like a cheat. It's not fair.

Carlos slid the napkin dispenser across the table to me, and I took one to cover my face.

"I don't talk about it." I took a deep breath and felt the ridges of my scars through my jeans. I stared at the ceiling, the floor, the donut case. Anywhere but at Carlos.

I didn't tell him how having me around reminds our mom and dad about what happened and makes everything worse. Mom doesn't talk to her friend Gilda anymore. They used to be really tight, and we haven't been back to her house. It's not Gilda's fault there was a bear in her yard. We stopped going to the festival too. In the hospital, the nurses and everyone would ask about my mom, "How's Vivian?" as if she was the one attacked. Carlos brought her flowers and tea.

"Did Dr. Wu have anything helpful to say?" Carlos looked so hopeful, I tried not to let my face show what I really thought. I told him how the doctor said our brains get caught in a loop and it makes it hard to heal and forget things. He told me to use all the senses I could when I woke up to help my brain feel like I was safe in my room, not in the brambles.

"I know it's not the same, like at all," Carlos said, "but I used to get really freaked out before tests in college. I'd wake up the day of the test in a pure panic. I told my favorite professor, and she said to think of something silly and it would calm me down. It worked—for me, at least. Could you write down the dream and shift what happens? Maybe add your own elements and change the ending." It sounded straight-up goofy, but I nodded anyway.

"Thanks, Carlos."

"For real, though, isn't there anyone else you can talk to about this? Ethan?"

"He worries a lot." If I told Ethan how bad it was, it would probably give him an ulcer.

Carlos took a breath to argue, but he blew it out again. He reached into his backpack. "Here you go. Sorry I didn't get it to you yesterday." He set a squishy present wrapped in old newspaper and blue ribbon on the table. Carlos works for an organization that tries to get companies to waste less stuff. He's always reusing things, like newspaper.

"What is this? Can I open it?"

"It's your birthday, boss." I tore the paper open down the back. It was a new blue hoodie, and it was the softest thing I'd ever felt.

"This is awesome. Thanks, Carlos."

"I noticed the one you wear all the time has a couple of holes," Carlos said.

My other hoodie was worn thin, and Mom had already sewed the seam and the wristband twice.

"I love you, Newt. Don't ever forget." He looked me in the eye. "You wanna get out of here?" He scooped up my napkins and dropped them in his empty coffee cup. I didn't feel ready, but we left anyway.

The thing about Carlos is, he's never in a hurry. When you're with him, you get time to look around and absorb the neighborhood. I like to count all the things they don't have on Murphy. Bus stops. Sushi places. A guy turning mangos into chile-dusted flowers. Signs for shoe stores, banks, and barbershops—all in Spanish. Carlos lived in the neighborhood, so it probably all felt normal to him. We stopped at the Farmacia Ramírez so he could pick up a prescription for abuela. He told Mrs. Ramírez it was my birthday, and she let me pick a treat off the shelf. I like salty stuff, so I grabbed some saladitos and thanked her. I offered Carlos one, and he saved it until he could eat it in a lemon.

Abuela's house was already full of people, cooking smells, and happy noise when we rolled up. My uncles were on the porch, arguing about whether or not Altuve was the best second baseman of all time. You never knock on abuela's door, you just walk inside. Unless you talk trash about Hernández, their favorite pitcher. If you do that, you run.

"What's up, Figgy? How's the leg?" My cousin Manny stood up from a card game to shake my hand and pull me into a hug. All the other cousins around the table did the same.

My aunts and grandma were in the kitchen, talking about ten things at once and cooking a feast. My stomach growled for the first time in forever. I couldn't keep the smile off my face. There's always a lot of yelling, but happy yelling, not arguing.

Carlos volunteered us to help in the kitchen, and we made

rice and beans and carnitas without any extra leafy stuff, goat cheese, or healthy seeds. Abuela liked to make a Mexican feast when the whole family was there. My grandma showed me how much oregano and onion and salt to add to the pozole.

"You gotta know how to cook. It's important," she said, like she does every time. My nina and tía Birdy carried a big pink box full of cake out of my grandma's bedroom. The cake said HAPPY BIRTHDAY, NEWTON!! on the top and ¡¡FELIZ CUMPLE NEWTON!! on the bottom in purple buttercream. My mainland family is so big, it takes two people to hold a cake and everybody else to worry they might drop it.

"It's chocolate with caramel," abuela whispered. "I know you like that kind." She gave me a good squeeze. There was nowhere to put the cake in the kitchen, so they laid it back on the bed under my abuela's Last Supper painting and told the kids to leave it alone.

My parents and Leti got there, and it was time to eat. I worried that they'd start telling everybody about Marvelo, but nobody said anything. Island stuff stays on the island.

My family sat along three tables, joined by tablecloths, that stretched from the living room to the dining room to the kitchen. I ate carnitas and nopales with tortillas until my stomach hurt. My aunts brought out the cake again, this time with candles, and when I blew them out, I wished that I could stay there in Lincoln forever. My piece just said NEW with a perfect buttercream rose. Leti doesn't like frosting, so I got one of her roses too. They sang to me, and I got a stack of birthday cards and some presents. My cousin Joe gives me a birthday card every year stuffed with stickers and magnets, the kind you get for free at stores. I don't know if he means it as a joke, or if he wants to give something but he doesn't have any money to spare. There are a lot of kids. I'm too shy to ask, so I just say thank you.

Afterward, Leti played chase with cousins and neighbor kids out front. I wandered around inside, because I like it when my aunts say how tall I am. Mom fixed a leaky faucet in the kitchen. She told my cousins they should come visit. They all made agreeing sounds, but nobody ever comes. It's hard to get out to the island, they say. I think this neighborhood is too comfortable for them to leave.

A basketball hit the window frame, and I almost jumped out of my shoes. Dad ran in and grabbed a beer, laughing at my tío Ed's trash talk about Carlos's jump shot. Leti stopped playing chase to join the basketball game. Even in her sandals, Leti scored a three-pointer off of Carlos in under a minute, and everybody cheered. My grandma waited for me back in the kitchen.

"Tell me how it went at that doctor Carlos found," she said.

I told her he had some good ideas, and she flopped back into her chair and crossed herself. She said she knew it would work, because she prayed. Dad and Leti pushed through the door all sweaty and laughing.

"I'm sorry, Mama. We gotta get back to the island."

Saying goodbye to everyone took almost an hour. My grandma gave Little Leti cake for the ferry, but I wasn't sure if I'd ever be able to eat again. Leti would probably eat hers before we got on the water. Rain splats dotted the driveway.

We climbed into the truck, and the engine rumbles covered up all the laughing and yelling in the house. Mom and Dad sang along with the radio.

"You're always in a good mood after we go to Lincoln," I said.

"Or maybe I'm in a good mood because now we get to go home." He smiled.

"How come you didn't tell them about Marvelo?" I said. Nobody had mentioned it all night. He waved his hand.

"They wouldn't believe me anyway." I didn't believe him either, but that didn't stop him from telling me. He patted my knee. "Meet me at the dock after school tomorrow. I've got a meeting with the foreman, and after that I'll bring your present."

"What is it?" Leti yelled.

"We're not telling," Mom said.

"Does it have wheels?" Leti said. They laughed.

"It might," Dad said, and I pictured my bike. Just like I wanted.

Leti fell asleep and snored. I put her leftover cake on the space between us before it could slide off her lap. I turned toward the window and pretended to sleep, but that was the last thing I wanted to do. I scraped paint off the door handle and thought about the party. Faraway mountains made the sky look like a cracked eggshell, breaking away from the earth. A big, dark mystery lay between the ocean and the broken-shell sky.

Halfway through the ferry ride, the engines slow down while the ferry cuts through a narrow channel between two uninhabited islands. Tree branches lean over and dim the stars. Every time it happens, I feel like we're going through a door between the real world and the island, but that night it felt like the door would close behind us and I'd be stuck on Murphy forever.

CHAPTER 3

On Monday, the principal from Lincoln Bay Middle School came to talk to us about going to school on the mainland. Some kids stay on Murphy, but most go to a school off the island after sixth grade. About two-thirds go to Lincoln Bay Middle School. A real yellow school bus shuttles them to and from the ferry terminal.

Murphy used to be a vacation destination. Truman Murphy got shipwrecked on the island over a hundred years ago and survived by eating berries and mussels until fishermen rescued him. He told them he had wrestled a bear, seen a lake monster, and dreamed of grand parties in the forest. He bought the island and made it like his dream. He built a hotel and added gardens, bandstands, and a zoo. A South African freighter delivered barrels full of live, psychedelic cichlids to Gertrude Lake. Tourists came for the fortune-tellers, circus performers, musicians, and confectioners. The island became a one-of-a-kind wonderland like nowhere else on earth. The resort closed after World War I, and Murphy became an artist colony. We don't get many tourists anymore, but most of the original buildings remain. Murphy School used to be the old main hotel, a casino, and a few cottages. A couple of the cottages were used for fortune-telling and séances. Now they're used for math and art.

Lincoln Bay Middle School looks just like a school in the movies. Kids eat in a lunchroom. There's a football field with bleachers. Murphy School has "island values." Mostly that means that we don't have a football team, but it's okay to go to school barefoot. Kids start kindergarten when they're "ready," not by their age. So our class has a couple of kids just turning eleven, and Lila Poe is practically fourteen. They teach home-steading here, like how to grow and can food. Mom visited Leti's third-grade class this year to talk about keeping goats and making soap and cheese. We don't have a basketball team either, and it bugs Leti. She wants to be a point guard. She's short, but if anyone can do it, she can.

You could tell that the new Lincoln Bay principal thought an old casino room was an odd place to have an assembly. She stared at the gold pillars, the fuzzy-red-swirl wallpaper, and the old pneumatic tubes that used to carry people's money somewhere safe. She set up a screen and showed us what a normal school looked like. Their assemblies are in an auditorium with a big fancy screen. Lincoln Bay has desks in rows and giant whiteboards. A lot of our classrooms have tables from the old dining halls, or people's kitchen castoffs.

The assistant principal talked about sports teams, the science lab, and all the extra stuff you get at a city school. When she brought up the drama club and the shows they perform, I nudged Ethan. A drama club is right up his alley.

"As if!" He put as much disgust into a whisper as he could. Ethan was signed up to return to Murphy School. Technically, you could stay all the way through high school, but the classes got smaller every year. Mom hadn't sent the form back yet, but I was planning to switch to Lincoln Bay. I used to want to stay too, but this year was different. Everything about Lincoln Bay was awesome. I wanted the lockers, the shiny linoleum floors, and nobody knowing the worst thing that ever happened to me.

The Lincoln Bay presentation was the best part of the day. After that, kids teased me about my dad spotting Marvelo. A kid named Abby made a crack for the twentieth time about my scars looking like a spiderweb. Ethan tried to get me to research moon snails with him for the brochure, but I had to figure out my own project. He might have forgotten my birthday present at home, but he did offer to share his chicken nuggets at lunch. I wasn't hungry, but I ate a couple anyway to be polite.

After school, I went home and took a nap like a pre-schooler. I've been doing it all year. I set the alarm to meet Dad but woke up from a dream before it went off. There is a hard, dark space between the bad dream and being awake and safe. I pressed my hands against the ache wrapped around the bones inside my knee, but that only made it worse. I knew I was safe in my bedroom, but something was off.

Someone stood beside my bed in the dim shadow from the door. I jumped and scooted toward the corner. My sister stood there, wearing the striped woolly hat with a pompom from my closet.

"What's going on, Leti?"

"Hey, Newt. I have a surprise for you." She leaned toward me, like a cat sneaking up on a butterfly.

"A birthday present?"

"That's on your desk," she said. "But also . . ." She pulled the pompom hat off. "I've got another eye, pal." A white circle with a crayon-brown iris and a wide pupil was taped to her forehead.

She pulled a necklace out from under her shirt with an eye-shaped milagro charm and tried to make scary noises. I slid my legs out of bed, but they wobbled. A bad dream can give me the shakes until I go back to bed and it starts all over again.

"Four eyes!" she yelled.

I laughed and grabbed the present off my desk: three books from the used bookstore by the bakery, with faded covers and crisp yellow pages that smelled like vanilla. Each cover had some extreme adventure—people lost in the wilderness, a guy trudging through snow, and boys on a raft pointed toward a waterfall.

"None of them have dogs that die," Leti said. "I asked. And I made you this." She held out a bookmark with NEWTON in big bubble letters. She'd used a different color for each letter and strung a ribbon through a hole punched in the top.

"This is really nice, Leti. Thank you. How'd you get it laminated?" I turned it over. She had signed the back in her best cursive. She's been working on her signature lately for letters to pen pals.

"I did it at school." She probably charmed the ladies in the office to let her use the laminating machine. Even though she's only nine, she's very persuasive. "Do you want to play a game? Or make some cinnamon toast? Do you want to make *me* some cinnamon toast?"

"Sure, give me a minute. You should put that milagro back before Mom gets home from work." She cackled and dropped my hat on the chair by the door on her way out.

After the attack, our mom started keeping a jar of milagro charms on the kitchen table for emergencies. Mom's tía Lucía is a curandera, a folk medicine doctor, in California. She gave Mom her first milagro, a little golden mule, when her family moved from Mexico to the States. Mom gives them away when someone has a problem. When she starts to run out, she asks Lucía to send more. Lucía sends novena candles too. After the attack, she tried to cure my feelings of susto over a video call on the computer. I didn't get fixed, but she sent bitter tea and creams to try too.

I sort the milagros sometimes when I'm avoiding homework. I look at the rough little faces on the people and the details on the animals. If a goat is sick, Mom wears a goat charm on a bright purple ribbon around her neck. If Dad goes fishing with Carlos, Mom adds a fish. She always wears a heart. It's worn down to a lump, but I remember what it looked like before.

Mom gave me a silver foot on a chain after the attack. It's not real silver; most are made from tin or something. She gave my grandma a golden eye for her cataracts. When Carlos joined the army and got deployed six years ago, Mom gave him a little house, so he would have good luck getting home.

I got a foot.

Mom got home from work as Leti and I were wrapping up cinnamon toast and Mastermind. I left to meet Dad. I took a shortcut to the dock, past the rusty Ferris wheel and the meadow where striped circus tents used to stand year-round.

Stories build up on Murphy Island, because they don't have anywhere to go. My parents told us all of them, all the wild island history, but most can't be true. I passed the flamingos by the spring pools. It's way colder here than in their native habitat, but they stay anyway.

The ferry grew as it crossed the channel and floated closer to Murphy. When I was younger, Mom told me the ferry shrank when it left so it wouldn't scare the fish as it sailed away. I thought it was magic.

I pictured my new bike. It probably had a carbon frame and disc brakes. I stopped to stretch my leg at the little free library by the side of the road. People drove by with blurry pity smiles, and I pretended to browse the books.

Maybe my bike would still be in the box, smelling like new tires and waiting to be assembled. *New* means it's only yours and none of the other Murphers will point out that it used to be theirs. No scratches or dings. The story starts when you get it. New is wonderful.

Mostly islanders and a couple of visitors got off the ferry, but not Dad. A few people waved. A line of cars rolled off. I kicked the gravel. The dock emptied, except for a woman and her poodle. She watched me, like she wanted me to leave, but I didn't. Finally, she sighed and signaled the poodle. He put his paws on the edge of the drinking fountain and licked the spout while she pushed the button.

"Good boy, Bosco," she said. I made a noise, and she shot me a look. "Are you waiting for the fountain?"

"No thanks," I said. She made a sour face, but the poodle looked apologetic.

A taco truck with a rooster painted on the side rolled off the dock ramp, and I saw Dad in his favorite baseball hat behind the wheel. He tapped the horn and came to a stop close enough for me to read the menu on the door.

"Hey, mijo! ¡Sorpresa!" He waved as the brakes squeaked.

"Hi! Is it in the back?"

"Is what in the back?" he said.

"My birthday present. You said you picked something up in Lincoln."

"Nobody has one of these on the island." He hopped out and patted the side of the truck like a horse. "Mira, I know it's intimidating, but your mom and I think it's best. You'll get the hang of it in no time."

"Get the hang of what?"

"Your new wheels!" He drew out the *e* so it sounded like *wheeeeeels*.

"Is the bike in the back?" I tried to see inside, but the window was too high, even on tiptoes.

"This is better than a bike." He gestured toward the truck. I still didn't get it. "If you bump into Marvelo on a bike, you could be a goner."

And then I got it.

"Are you kidding? You got me a taco truck?!" I yelled. He nodded.

"It *was* a taco truck, back in the day. The way Conci did al pastor was dynamite! The truck has been hibernating for a while. Cool, no?"

"I'm thirteen. *Thirteen.* I'm not old enough for a license. I'm barely allowed to go to the movies without an adult. What am I going to do with this?" I pointed, but it was like Dad and I were looking at two different things.

"You can learn. Don't take it off the island, but it can get you around and to the ferry. It's safe for you to drive around here."

"What if I hit someone, or drive into the water? This is dangerous!"

Dad scratched his head and looked at me. "Yeah, it's tricky until you get the hang of it. I already hit the roof on a street sign," he said. I stared at him as hard as I could. If it's possible to stare sense into somebody, it would have happened then. "Look, Newt—I want you to have unique wheels. We know it's hard for you to get around sometimes." He gestured toward my leg but didn't look at it. "Summer is about to start, and now with Marvelo . . . People have spotted him out of the water before. And maybe you're not ready for a bike, you know? Your leg is still healing. Your mom wanted you to have something big and safe."

"One person. One pretty unreliable person thought *maybe* she saw it out of the water." My parents' friend Brenda is nice, but she can't see that well, and she likes drama. "The doctor said a bike would help my leg."

"Your mom will be happy." He looked at me. "She wanted to get you a golf cart. If you go to school on the mainland, you'll need some wheels to the ferry, and most days I leave for work too early to take you. A bike won't help you if it's raining. I was on my way to see a guy, and I stopped at Billy's. He bet me I couldn't walk around the truck on my hands. So of course I won. I won *this*!" He slapped the rooster again and smiled with as much pride as I've ever seen him wear. Dad took a gymnastics class in high school. His parents could only afford for one of them to go, so he taught his brothers and sisters all the handstands and flips he learned. He's got moves, when he's not sore from carrying drywall.

"Kids can't drive." I leaned toward him. "Won't I get arrested?"

"Who's going to arrest you? Deputy Pat? I talked to him. He says whatever it takes to help you feel safe." I curled my fingers into fists until my nails pressed into my palms.

"I feel safe already." When I was awake, anyway. "I wanted

a bike. Just a normal bike," I said, like he didn't know. My frown reflected back at me in the big window down the side of the truck above the rooster. A rusty ladder stretched up the back.

He handed me keys with a bright blue rabbit's foot, like no actual bunny ever.

"Don't you have something to say?"

I choked out a thanks and walked behind the truck. My life never stopped being weird. I sniffled and he pretended not to hear.

"We can use the money we would have spent on the golf cart for the new water heater," he said. It took two tries for Dad to get the back doors open, and they groaned like they might fall off. "You can put your stuff back here. But not too much stuff, right, because the gas mileage isn't great. And you gotta be super careful going downhill and turning. It's top-heavy."

I sat on the bumper and hung my head. "I've never even driven a go-kart!" My heart beat against my back. I expected the truck to smell like burritos, but it smelled like lemon cleaner and incense. Silver cupboards and loose wires lined both sides. Duct tape crisscrossed the seat. Green fuzzy dice hung from the rearview mirror.

"Time to learn how to drive." Dad clapped me on the back. I didn't move. "A bike wouldn't even break twenty going up the hill."

I climbed into the passenger seat, but he pushed me into the driver's seat. I wasn't sure what to do after that. The seat was obviously made for someone bigger than me. Dad moved it forward so I could reach the pedals. I couldn't find where the key went. Dad buckled up and showed me the ignition. They gave Carlos an old Mini when he turned seventeen, after he had a driver's license. If he hit anything, there wouldn't be too much damage. I got a tank.

I don't know if it made it easier or not, but the steering wheel was extra large. "So many possibilities!" Dad said, and double-checked his seat belt. "Pull the stick down to D. That's for 'drive.'" Dad pointed at the gearshift, like driving a car should ever be that easy.

"D for 'disaster,'" I mumbled, but he didn't hear me over the engine. "Please don't make me do this!" The words scratched my throat, but he pretended not to hear.

"The brake is on the left. The gas is on the right." That was his driving lesson. "P is for 'park,' D is for 'drive,' R for 'reverse,' and you don't have to worry about the one or the two." N was for 'neutral,' which meant the truck wouldn't go unless it was on a hill. Somebody had painted an X over the R with blue nail polish. "Try not to get in a spot where you have to reverse," Dad said.

I drove around the empty parking lot by the dock to get used to moving my foot from one pedal to the other without looking down, which is harder than it sounds. The ferry left for the mainland again, and the chance of plowing down the ramp into the water made my hands sweat and slip off the wheel. I hit a bush, but I didn't hit the streetlight or the guys on unicycles.

"You're ready," Dad said. I wasn't, but I pulled out of the lot onto Evers Road. Driving down the street felt easier, which I'm sure isn't right. The engine sounded as if there was a giant motorcycle in the back, so I couldn't even hear if I knocked off some poor parked car's side mirror. Sound blasted up through holes in the floor, like someone had shot at the truck from below. The holes were smaller than bottle caps but big enough to see the street whizzing past. Every time a car came from the other direction, my stomach burned. I gave my dad a dirty look at a stop sign, but he stared through the windshield.

"Why did you say you saw it?" I said when I got to a straight part of the road. He knew the "it" I meant.

"Because I did," he said. I peeled my eyes off the road to glance at him.

"Nobody believes you," I said. "It's so embarrassing. Can't you just say you made it up? For your book or something?"

"I didn't."

"Dad!" I yelled. "Come on! Please."

"Watch the road," he said. There are big things all around Murphy. Whales close enough to the island that they look like smooth rocks, just for a minute, before they dunk down into the blue again. Sea lions. Redwoods with trunks wider than a car. But not Marvelo. Because this is still real life on earth and not a late-night monster movie.

"You're doing great. Pull over. We can work on Marvelo and Manxadon at the lake," he said.

"No thanks," I said.

"Then we can keep practicing, wise guy." We drove around the island loop and slowly through town. We didn't go around Fitz Beach, where everyone hangs out, or past the spring pools. He explained laws and rules while I turned left and right and tried not to die. Who goes first at a stop sign? What do the yellow triangles mean? There were a hundred things I never thought about before, and he covered them all.

"You've got this. Try not to get noticed," he said, right after he gave me a giant shiny truck and told me to drive it around. Everything rattled in the back. My seat squeaked around curves like an old ship rocking in the waves.

"If you could go anywhere right now, where would you go?" Dad asked.

"Abuela's house," I said.

"No, you can never take this off the island. But if you could drive somewhere on the island, where would it be?"

I turned right. I knew exactly where I wanted to go.

CHAPTER 4

After dropping Dad off down the street at his friend Tom's house, I went straight to Ethan's house. He opened his front door and held out a long, lumpy package in green-striped tissue paper.

"Happy belated birthday! You're going to love it," he said.

I tore off the paper. "Are these bowling pins?"

"You know what they are. They're your very own juggling clubs! I'll teach you how to juggle for the festival!" I held them out and smiled, because he waited for me to do it. I used to want juggling clubs. I played with his and he tried to teach me tricks, but it wouldn't ever stick because I didn't have my own to practice with.

He wanted us to have a new act for the Marvelo Festival, which is on the summer solstice, right after school ends. It's a big vaudeville show to celebrate the "creative nature of the island." My parents volunteered with the festival as soon as they moved here. Mom danced, sang, and helped Gilda organize the whole thing. Both my parents built sets. The hardware store where my mom works donates wood and chicken wire and anything else needed. While they worked, Leti and I helped set up chairs and sweep. It was my favorite family thing.

When we were eight, Ethan and I begged Gilda to let us do terrible card tricks in the show. I think we became friends because I was the only one in our class who would watch him butcher magic tricks over and over. His sleight of hand was terrible.

We performed every year. Last year, we were supposed to do a comedy act: we were going to be marathon runners in slow motion, and things kept going wrong before we got to the finish line. We planned to wear Ethan's dad's old neon running shorts, with wires sewed in so it would look like we were going so fast, the wind was blowing them backward. It's funnier than it sounds, and it took a lot of practice, but our act got canceled when I couldn't be there.

"Thanks for the present, no thanks on the juggling," I said.

"Come on. You have great aim," he said. We used to play basketball with Carlos's old hoop behind the garage. Now Leti was the only one who used it. "What else did you get?"

I told him about the books I got from Leti, the hoodie from Carlos, and the extra-soft pajama pants and bakery gift card I got from my parents. "One more. Come outside." I walked out to the sidewalk and pointed at the truck. "That is also a birthday present. From my parents. I'm not even joking."

"Wait, what? What's that for?"

"To drive. My dad gave it to me today at the dock."

"Incredible," he said. "Can I drive it?" He ran his hand over the rooster.

"No."

"Want to go down to the lake and look for Marvelo?" he said. I groaned.

"Not even a little bit." I adjusted my pant leg so it would stop rubbing against the scars. "You know he made it up."

"Maybe not. Let's ask my mom if you can get a spin on the wheel for your birthday! And then drive to the beach? Something might've washed up from the storm." I already said no to letting him drive, the festival, and the lake, so I agreed.

I have never met a kid who wanted to be rich as badly as Ethan. It started a few years ago, after his dad died when we were in second grade. He used to beg his mom to let him buy lottery tickets with his allowance. We look for treasure a lot. Fossils, Murphy's secret hidden emeralds, anything. I used to like it more when we were younger, when I thought we might actually find something. Ethan makes me check my coins for old ones when I get change, but I only have a few valuable ones memorized. A 1944 steel wheat penny, for example, will get you one hundred thousand dollars. Ethan says there could be one floating around, waiting for some lucky kid to find it. The chances of that happening—well, it's easier to go along with it.

We headed back to Ethan's mom's office, which was his sister's room before she joined the Peace Corps. When Ethan was obsessed with the lottery, his mom made a big scrap-wood wheel with lots of wedges, like a giant rainbow pie. Most wedges are blank, but some have "$1" or "$2" or "$5" written on them. The wheel also has four $25 sections, two spots to win $50, and one amazing, gold-glitter-covered $100 section. His mom thought we would look at the wheel and realize the terrible odds, but we were hooked. For $1, we could spin the wheel. It was a private lottery for Ethan and me.

"Mom, it's Newt's birthday," Ethan said. Beth looked up from her book and smiled, like she felt proud that I made it through another year.

"Happy birthday, Newt," she said. "That's 4,745 days on the planet, or about the lifespan of a nutria."

"What's a nutria?" I asked. Beth wins a lot of trivia nights at the People's Pub.

"A pretty big rodent," she said. "Crocodiles live about that long too, but you're just getting started, Newton Gomez!"

"Mom." Ethan rolled his eyes. "Can we spin the wheel for Newt's birthday?" It sat at the top of a bookcase behind her bowl chair.

"Do you have any money?" she said.

"Mom. Come on. We've only ever won seven dollars!" We split our winnings and spent it on small mochas at the Sunflower Café. "We cleaned your car *and* made a lemonade stand two weekends in a row, and you took all our money!" Fifty-two dollars. We bought fifty-two spins.

"I didn't take your money. That's how you chose to spend it. And then I chose to get a delicious pizza and some books."

"So give us a couple of freebies," Ethan said, and I nodded.

"Sorry, gentlemen. The gambling commission is cracking down." She went back to reading. I called my dad, and he said it was fine to drive to the beach if we were careful.

"I knew you'd love it once you got over the shock," he said. Thankfully he hung up before I had to answer. Ethan grabbed his dad's old tennis shoes and hopped into the passenger seat.

"Put your seat belt on," I said. I adjusted the mirror. "Did it click?"

"Didn't you hear it click?"

"Let me just test it." I reached toward his seat belt, but he slapped my hand away. "I just want to make sure I won't kill you." I tried to pull it again.

"Get off! It's fine, see?" He yanked the belt. "Let's go!"

Most people like the beaches on the west side of the island, around Shallow Bay and Jamila Park, because the water is calm and better for swimming, but I drove in the other direction. Echo Beach is good for crabs, anemones, and being alone. And in theory, finding fossils.

We both stayed quiet until we pulled off near Ethan's favorite bluff. I forgot to pull the gear knob to *P* when I stopped. The truck lurched into a driftwood log, *clunk-clunk-clunk*ed, and died.

"All in all, that wasn't bad," Ethan said, but his eyes were buggy and his skin looked pale.

I got out, took deep breaths, and read the menu painted under the window. The truck had served everything from turkey tamales to tripe tacos. Some of it sounded good, but since I had their truck now, maybe it wasn't.

Ethan changed into his dad's shoes. He says they have better grip to climb the bluff. I think he just wants a part of his dad close by. He had to wait a long time before the shoes would fit. He kept them by his desk for years.

"Remember, mammoth tusks are more curved, mastodon

tusks are straighter," Ethan said as we crunched through gravel and mussel shells to the sand.

"I know."

"And *mastodon* literally means 'nipple tooth,' because someone thought it looked like a brick with boobs," Ethan said, and I nodded. He tells me that every time. We poked around the roots and rocks on the bluff. I closed my eyes and took deep breaths of ocean air. It smells better on Echo Beach than anywhere else on the island. It's like taking a long drink when you're thirsty.

You can always tell how high the tide came in overnight by the line of beach junk. It's mostly driftwood, kelp, and broken crab shells. This time, the tide swept the junk all the way to the woods. It felt peaceful and unsettled, like walking into a room right after a fight ends. The sand we walked on had been covered in twenty-foot swells of angry ocean. Now the beach was smooth and clean of everything but sea-foam, bird tracks, and us.

"Remember when we did the act with the giant shadow puppets on the big white sheets? That was awesome," Ethan said. He scratched his cheek and looked at me. "I can't wait to get back to the festival this year. Gilda said I could do some ring magic, but I didn't want to do it without you."

Ethan scooped up a handful of wet sand and held it up to his face. He says there's a million dollars in gold dust on the beach. He's been trying to figure out how to get it out for years. "Things are better now, right?" Ethan's voice got higher. "The festival is a month away. You can learn to juggle with the clubs. We'll make an act, and you'll love being back. You'll see."

"I'm not doing it anymore. For real, Ethan. You can sign up. I'll watch from the audience." He wanted everything to be like it used to be, but the last place I wanted to be was back onstage.

I knew he was nervous about the Lincoln Bay assembly. The kids who go to school on the mainland usually don't do the festival, because commuting to Lincoln makes it hard to rehearse. But if I got back up onstage, they would only see me as *that* kid, the one who almost died picking berries. Even if I wore a costume, they'd be looking for the scars and feeling pity. I wouldn't get the warm, fuzzy feeling I used to get from the stage lights, because part of me would know that the audience was distracted by what they couldn't even see. Ethan picked up an old purple toy car half-buried in the sand and put it in his pocket. I used to love playing with cars. But that didn't mean I would play with them now, and I wasn't signing up for the festival either. I dragged my feet in wavy lines toward the trees.

There was something big hidden in the shadows near the tree line, past the washed-up junk. Usually the big somethings are tree stumps. Once a wooden crate of mangos fell off a ship and spilled out all over the beach. Sometimes a stump turns out to be a napping sea lion, but they usually stay in the sun. "Look." We climbed over smooth gray logs to investigate.

A bear. It was a bear.

Not another real live bear. Someone had carved a wooden bear, a little smaller than me, out of a log. It felt like I got punched right below the ribs.

This was a joke. A mean joke to freak out the bear-attack kid. The kid who dreamed about it so much, his big brother made him go to an appointment with a special doctor.

Ethan pushed sea cabbage off the bear's face with a stick. Little whiskers on its snout and the top of its head looked as fluffy as wood could. Shiny emerald-green eyes sat between two round ears. It held a Y-shaped piece of wood up to its chest in a clawed paw. The other arm hung down, half-covered in barnacles. Ethan took a step toward me, like he thought I might fall over.

"You didn't put this here as, like, a prank, right?" I said. I could tell by his face that he hadn't. My breath wheezed like it needed grease.

"Dude, no! Someone probably left it too close to the beach and the storm caught it. It might've come from Lincoln, or San Francisco, or Timbuktu. Is that near an ocean?"

I leaned against a tree and took deep breaths to wash away

the nausea. I looked up so I wouldn't have to see it. The storm had thrown bull kelp into the tree branches all around me. It swung in the wind above my head like I was underwater. I held my breath, closed my eyes, and felt the rough bark against my back.

"Newt, you're all sweaty. Dude. That would be a mean joke." Ethan put his hand on my shoulder, like I might float away. "I'd never do that. It got pushed up on the tide. If someone put it in the water on purpose, it would probably disappear out to sea." I checked the wet sand around the bear, but the only footprints were ours and scratchy tracks from curious gulls. We were alone, except for the bear.

"Let's take it," Ethan said.

"No!"

"Maybe it's valuable. Check out what he's got in his hand. Paw. It looks like a wishbone," Ethan said. I didn't want to look at it. "We could make a wish. Maybe it's magic!"

"It looks like a slingshot. Come on." I practically had to drag him down the beach, and he complained the whole way.

We climbed into the front seat, and I started the truck. I moved the gearshift to *R* for "reverse" and stepped on the gas so we could ease back from the log. The engine chugged and hummed, but it didn't move.

I found out the hard way why someone would give a truck to a guy who could walk on his hands. I spotted Dad's handwriting on an old envelope by my feet, next to the *X* painted over the *R* on the gearshift display: "You might have to play around to get it to reverse. Maybe ask the shop teacher at school?" He drew a truck with a frowny face. We don't have a shop teacher at school. We don't have a shop.

Eventually I put the truck in *N,* and Ethan and I pushed on the front grille until the truck rolled, farther than it should have, down the hill before I jumped inside.

"Whoa! Whoa!" Ethan yelled. He ran, holding the bumper, like that might slow it down. I stomped on the brake, and Ethan hit his face on the grille.

"Ethan! Are you all right?" I remembered to shift into *P* when I stopped. I found some old rooster napkins in the glove box for his bloody nose. "I'm sorry."

He held the napkins over his face the whole way home.

"I doe you dibbit bean too," he said through the napkins. I laughed, he laughed, and his nose started bleeding all over again.

CHAPTER 5

After I took Ethan home, everything felt different. All the good feelings left, and I didn't want to drive anymore. I felt sick and tired. I shook the big dumb steering wheel and yelled. Not words, just noise, like my mouth was a staticky radio on full volume. I yelled until my head ached. I hadn't asked for any of this. I didn't want to have to worry about crashing the truck, or finding bears, or going to sleep. A kid shouldn't have to worry about just falling asleep.

I pulled over on the way to pick up Dad and turned off the engine. I left the keys in the ignition and got out to walk. Dad could take it back. The first couple blocks were fine, but my leg shook going uphill on the third. I tripped on a tree root and knew I wouldn't make it all the way home. I headed back to the silver danger-box-on-wheels and kicked it before climbing back inside.

I thought about the wooden bear, waiting at the beach. Anytime I went back, there he would be. "It's just beach junk," I said. But I didn't want any junk on Echo Beach. It was one of the few places left on the island where I didn't worry about anything. Nobody was around to see my leg. It was just Ethan, me, and the crabs. I didn't want to let a stupid wooden bear ruin it.

I drove back to the beach. A girl I didn't recognize was digging a hole by my favorite log. Her faded jacket blended into the wood. We don't get many new kids on Murphy. Tourists from the mainland usually wear bright clothes and floppy hats, thinking Murphy is warm and tropical just because it's an island. It was still a few weeks until summer, definitely jacket weather. The girl looked almost local, but she wasn't. I might not be friends with everyone, but I still know them all. Even the homeschooled kids.

She looked my age, but she had a bun like my grandma wears, if my grandma used moss-covered sticks to hold a bun together, which she totally would never.

"Did you lose something?" I pointed to the pile of sand.

"I'm looking for clams. I don't know if I'm doing it right," she said. Dad and I used to go crabbing and clamming all the time to stock up for chowder and steamers and crab cakes. He loves crab cakes, but we haven't been since before the attack.

She dusted sand off a manila clam and plunked it into her bucket.

"Those are really good in chowder. Or as steamers, if you like those."

She looked at me like she'd forgotten I was there. "Nice beach."

"It's pretty perfect," I said. Almost. I could see the wooden bear near the woods. Waiting.

"You live here?" she asked. I nodded. "Lucky."

"Not really. Are you on summer vacation already?" The mainland schools always finished first.

"Yeah. It's amazing here. I'm Izzy. What's your name?"

"Newt."

"Is that a nickname?" Two more manilas in the bucket.

"It's short for Newton. But don't call me Fig."

"Why . . . Oh." Izzy nodded and the sticks in her hair clacked together. She crinkled her nose. "That's not very funny." I smiled and she smiled back the way you'd smile at a little kid. "People used to call me Fizzy at my old school."

"I'm sorry. . . . I'm the only one with that kind of name. My brother is Carlos, and my sister is named Leti," I said. "It's short for Leticia. She might be a writer, a basketball player, or an evil genius. My dad says it's too soon to tell."

Izzy kept raking, two cockles and a softshell, and I kept talking. "She's named after my aunt. Carlos's name is actually Eduardo, who's another uncle, but it wasn't enough to be named after one uncle, so he's named after two. I'm named after Isaac Newton, because my mom read a book about him while she was pregnant with me. My dad thought naming me after a scientist might make me grow up to be one. I told him they could name me after a volcano, but it won't make me explode."

She raked and dug and threw rocks to the side without looking up. I could feel my face getting red.

"What did your dad say about the volcano?"

"He said I was thinking like a scientist already."

"And if you were a girl?"

"Florence, after Florence Bailey. She was a bird scientist. But they must have given up on the experiment, because they named Leti after someone they actually know who sends birthday cards." I twisted my foot in the sand.

"I'm going to look her up. My favorite scientist is Jane Goodall or Biruté Galdikas." I tried to look like I knew who she was talking about, but she laughed. "Goodall's a chimpanzee expert, and Galdikas is an orangutan expert." Izzy's eyes flicked down to the tracks of pink scars from my calf to my thigh, but she looked straight back up to my eyes.

"Nice talking to you," I said. I waved and walked toward

the bear without looking back. I grabbed it on two spots where the barnacles had rubbed off. When I pulled it, I almost fell back into a tree.

I wouldn't be able to move it by myself. And if I couldn't move it, it could be here for weeks until someone else took it or the tide rose that high again.

I tried to hide my limp as I walked back toward Izzy. She found ten more clams in the time it took me to cross the sand.

"My friend and I found a bear statue when we were here earlier," I said. "I want to get it off the beach and find its owner. Would you mind helping me? It's kind of heavy." She put the rake inside the bucket with the clams and moved it away from the water. I pointed at the bear shape near the trees. She stood up and matched my pace. She didn't say anything about how slowly I went. We got to the bear, and she squatted down next to it.

"I've seen these before. My grandma has one just like it." Izzy looked closer.

If we couldn't find its owner, I'd chuck it in a dumpster. Or run it over with the truck.

We dragged it out of the trees, but its waterlogged body weighed a ton. Sand scratched the tight skin around my scars. I got splinters under my nails.

"We could just roll it back into the surf, and the ocean could take it back," I said.

"It's better to find the owner. Somebody probably misses it, and it's not far."

We fell over a lot and dropped it a couple of times. My shorts turned to sandpaper, and I ached all over by the time we got back to the truck. I opened the back doors and climbed inside. The whole truck groaned and wobbled. Izzy stayed outside. I stood the bear in the corner, wedged in where maybe a stove used to be.

A blue heron stood in the water down the shore, waiting for a fish with bad luck to swim between its pipe-cleaner-thin legs.

"This is your truck?" Izzy looked around, from the giant steering wheel to the fuzzy dice to the grimy window. I could've lied, but I nodded. She squinted at me. "How old are you?"

"Thirteen."

"Me too. Almost fourteen. But I don't have a truck." She traced the outline of the bear's slingshot, or wishbone, or whatever. "I don't mean to be rude, but how are you driving around?"

I tried to think of an easy answer, but she didn't wait. "I'm glad I got to see him. Thank you." She smiled and headed back to her clam bucket.

I waited until she went back to digging before I stretched my leg so it would stop feeling like it was on fire. I massaged my knee with shaky hands. I closed my eyes, but I could still feel the bear there.

If it granted wishes like Ethan thought, I wouldn't want a bike, or a birthday redo, or anything else. I would wish to be off Murphy Island. The truck, and the bear, and the parts of the island where I don't go anymore without smelling broken leaves and feeling raw—that could all get smaller and smaller as I rode away on the ferry. I'd miss the part when they disappeared, because I would never look back again.

CHAPTER 6

Wednesday afternoon, Ethan walked into our kitchen with a huge smile on his face. "I have something to tell you," he said. He paced around the table, where I was doing homework. "You know the bear's wishbone?"

"The slingshot?"

He straightened the Sacred Heart over the sink. Ethan noticed all the Virgins of Guadalupe that Mom keeps around the house the first time he came over. I've never been to Mexico, but our house looks like pictures of it. I mean, Murphy houses are all odd, but they are odd in a lot of the same ways. One person hangs up wind chimes made from old kitchen whisks and wooden spoons, and five other houses do it. Ideas spread around the island like goat hair in the wind.

But our place is different. Mom painted the entryway hot pink and hung up a Virgin of Guadalupe right across from the door. Most of the other houses have white walls. My parents like color, and Mom gets a discount on paint at the hardware store where she works. The other rooms are all different colors, and you can find Virgins and candles in almost every single one. The Virgin by the door has a bowl on the bottom that used to have holy water in it, but now it has heather, because Chuck drank the holy water and Mom says in Scotland heather brings good luck. There's a big wall of photos in the dining room with about a million cousins, aunts, uncles, and grandparents. Roses that dried out before I was even born hang over doorways. I told Dad once that it looked like we tried to be more Mexican, but he said all that stuff helps them to remember that we are. Our house makes up for the 99 percent of the island that isn't Latinx.

Most people stop in the hall, like they have to get ready to take it all in. But the first time Ethan came over, he walked around right away, checking everything out. I tried to show him a new model kit my brother got me, but he was staring at a Virgin standing on clouds, looking down on a papier-mâché world.

"Do you believe in heaven?" he said. I think he wanted me to say yes. It hadn't been that long since his dad had died. My parents had warned me not to ask about it.

"I'm not sure," I said.

"Do you go to Saint Benedict's for Mass? My dad took us sometimes." He looked at the novena candles and statues on a shelf above the table.

"We don't really go to church, apart from weddings and stuff," I said, and he looked confused. I shrugged.

"I can't explain my family," I said, and that he understood. His house has candles too, and crystals and pyramids to supposedly help you meditate.

I shook the old memories out of my head and opened the refrigerator. "My mom made tamales," I said, because they're his favorite. He picked out a chicken adobo tamal and a cheese one. Ethan didn't eat much after his dad died. He didn't talk much either. He ate tamales when he came over the first time, though, so I asked my grandma to teach me how to make them. I took my busted-up tamales to his house. I think he ate them to be polite, but at least he ate something.

Now I was the one who hardly ate anything. He offered me his bowl, but I shook my head. The cheese used to be my favorite, but they tasted mealy to me these days. I got a glass of water instead.

"I went back to the beach to look for the bear, but it was gone!" Ethan said.

"Oh yeah?"

"Don't even try it, Newt. I saw the drag marks to the parking lot. I checked your truck on a hunch. It was unlocked, so I climbed inside and made a wish on the bear's wishbone," he said. He took a third tamal.

"You hate wishes."

"No way. You're the one who can never decide what you want. You get freaked out about wishing for the wrong thing. Remember when we had that cakewalk at the carnival? You won, but you couldn't pick a cake. By the time we went back at the end, they were gone, and you almost cried."

There had been a decent chocolate cake, but there was a peanut butter cake too, with big whips of frosting. I hadn't tried peanut butter cake before, and I worried I wouldn't like it. In the end, both were gone and there was only a carrot cake like a brick, and something green that looked like preschoolers had made it.

"I didn't almost cry over cake. And bear statues don't grant wishes. That's ridiculous," I said as Margie the goat pulled the screen door open and came into the kitchen. It's Mom's fault. The first time Margie came inside, Mom was making vegetable soup. It was an all-you-can-eat buffet of veggie scraps. My grandma from Lincoln saw the goats in the house the last time she came to visit. Margie and Buster came in the kitchen, and Mom made them a salad. My grandma was horrified.

"A magic bear isn't any more ridiculous than candles, or meteors, or throwing money into a wishing well. People do it anyway! There's something special about that bear. I had to wish, in case it worked."

Margie headed for the hall, but I pushed her back outside and latched the screen door.

"I needed to do an experiment, a wish that wasn't too much, or that wouldn't turn into something terrible. Newt, you should lock the truck. Anybody can climb right in."

"When were you in the truck?"

"Last night," he said.

"So you came over but didn't knock or anything. Then you broke into the truck—"

"You make it sound like I broke the window or something. I opened the truck door. I had to hurry in case you found the owner."

"I made a flyer. I'm going to put it all over town. Did you break the wishbone wood?"

"No! I just stood in front of it," he said. "I couldn't decide what to wish for! Something that couldn't turn into a giant marshmallow man, you know? You've seen the movie, right?"

"Sure, everyone's seen it." I had no idea what he was talking about.

"I chewed it over for, like, twenty minutes. I want a pet, but maybe if I wished for a cat, then a mountain lion would show up on the beach." Animals swim over to Murphy from the mainland all the time. Not just bears. Deer, foxes, and mountain lions too. The big carnivores get returned to their natural habitats. We have a few fox families, and deer that graze all over. They're smaller than mainland deer, like living on an island gives them less space to grow. The Murphy Council says to let them fend for themselves, but people put out salt licks, leave apples on their trees in the fall, and put corn out in the winter.

Ethan tossed his corn husks into the compost bin. "Anyway, I wished for a hedgehog. It's small, pretty easy to take care of—and it's cute enough that my mom would say yes when I asked for it. They can be grouchy, but they don't stink. We've never had one." He smiled and bounced on his toes as if *he'd* won a cakewalk.

"So . . . you got a hedgehog?"

"No. My mom said one bit her once and she didn't think I would clean its cage," he said. I raised my eyebrows. "I'm not done, Fig. I got annoyed, so I took a hike." He paced. "I was in the cove, scratching around in the dirt for a harpoon or something, thinking about what we'll do over summer break. I heard twigs cracking under the hedge by the benches. It could have been a raccoon, or a squirrel, but it wasn't!"

"Was it a hedgehog? A giant, twig-cracking hedgehog?"

Ethan rolled his eyes and walked out of the kitchen. The front door opened. I got up to apologize, but I heard the chickens squawk and toenails *click-clack*ing over the hardwood floor in the living room. My stomach flopped. I pictured a giant hedgehog with quills like skewers, but Ethan came back carrying two boxes and a rope leash connected to a long dog. It looked like a black-and-white basset hound crossed with a chow, basically a panda bear with short legs and a long, wagging tail.

"That's not a hedgehog."

"Nope, that's a hedge*DOG,*" Ethan said. "You got mail." He put the boxes down on the table with two letters from Leti's pen pals. The biggest box was for my mom from somewhere called Pete's Plumes, and the other was for Leti and me from our grandma. I knew it had a ball for Chuck, and probably cookies or banana bread for us. Maybe pictures or a little money. I didn't tell Ethan what it was, because he would scarf all the treats.

"A hedge*dog*? That's not a thing."

"Exhibit A. It came out of the hedges! The bear gave me a hedgeDOG."

"Couldn't it be a bush dog? Or a bramble dog?"

"It was the hedge. The tall one that's trimmed around the sides to be a rectangle and everything. That's a hedge. Before you ask, I looked for his owner. Nobody is missing a dog." I nodded. It's easy to find a lost pet on an island.

"Where did he come from?"

"The hedges, dude. He's a hedgedog. I can get him a spiky collar, and he'll have quills! Hey, maybe I'll tell your dad, and he can be Marvelo and Manxadon's new apprentice! What do you think about Boxwood for a name? It's a type of hedge. I looked it up." He sat on the floor, and the dog climbed into his lap.

"Don't you think it's a coincidence? You could have found him anyway, not because you broke into my truck and made a wish?"

"Probably, but look at the evidence. I found him on the beach in a hedge. He's not an island dog, and somebody would've seen him if he came over with a mainlander. Your bear is granting wishes," Ethan said. "Maybe he could be in the festival with us. He could do tricks!"

"Maybe with you." People trained animals for festival acts, but those acts didn't always work out. Two years ago, a guy said he could get eight cats to balance on beach balls, but they freaked out when they saw the audience. Two balls popped and deflated. He gave Ethan and me twenty dollars to help round them up after the show.

We took Boxwood to the backyard and introduced him to Chuck and the goats. Chuck tried to play chase with him, but after Margie headbutted Boxwood into the fence, he just wanted to sit by Ethan.

"Look, he's smart," Ethan said. I couldn't believe that this panda dog was what Ethan had wished for. Ethan thought he had a little magic for once, and he used it to get a pet.

"How's it going studying the moon snails?" I said.

"I picked them as kind of a joke, but they're amazing! Their pale-pink shells are as big as grapefruit, but they can't fit their weird pudding bodies inside. They have seven rows of teeth that can drill holes in clamshells for lunch. Seven!" Meat rocks.

"Gross."

"What's your topic?"

"Tide pools," I said.

"That's too easy."

"You love tide pools. Remember when we found those shark egg cases?" I remembered how they looked like seed-pods until we held one up to the light and saw the little baby shark inside.

"If you help me clean the chicken coop, I'll let you take the eggs," I said, but he was already heading for the door.

"I gotta go home. Thanks for the tamales! Go make a wish."

"There's no such thing as a magic bear."

"My wish came true. You should wish for something before somebody claims the bear."

I laughed. Ethan glared at me, but I couldn't help it. I laughed until I howled, because the idea that a wooden bear could give Ethan a dog was nuttier than peanut butter cake.

CHAPTER 7

I hung lots of flyers on my way to the ferry after school on Thursday. They said FOUND: BEAR STATUE, with our phone number and address. My cousin David picked me up in Lincoln, and we met up with Manny and Carlos at Carlos's apartment to play video games. We stopped when we heard the raspado guy's cart bell outside. I got mango and Carlos got jamaica. We don't have a raspado guy on the island, but I could get shaved-ice drinks all the time once I'm at Lincoln Bay. We crunched ice all the way to the best comics shop in town.

I used to be super into comics, before it happened. The comics shop was one of my favorite things. My cousin Manny loves it, and Dad too, obviously. We don't have a comics shop on Murphy either, but they get them sometimes at the used-book store. When I was in the hospital, people brought me loads of comics. Old ones, new ones, all the series out of order, and more copies of comics I already had. We took them home, two boxes' worth, but I haven't read them. I stopped working on Marvelo and Manxadon with Dad too.

Carlos offered to buy me a couple comics, and I tried to look excited. I picked up the two most recent issues of *Scrapper Pang.* I didn't care if Scrapper would be able to salvage whatever he needed to save the augals on the dying planet, but letting Carlos buy the comics made him happy.

We took a bouquet of roses and carnations to my grandma, but she was out. I left them on her porch by a pot of geraniums with a mushy thank-you note in Spanish. She loves that stuff.

On the way back to the ferry, I asked Carlos to drive past Lincoln Bay Middle School. A kid drove a radio-controlled car around the empty parking lot.

"Was it amazing?" I said.

"What?"

"Middle school!"

The marquee out front said HAVE A GREAT WEEKEND, BULL-DOGS! like they were all one big team.

"It was ten years ago. Middle school isn't amazing. It's middle school, bro." Carlos laughed and tapped along to the radio on the steering wheel.

"Mom wants me to stay at Murphy School, but I want to go

to Lincoln Bay like you did. I'm going to ask them if I can try staying with abuela so it's easier." Carlos raised his eyebrows.

"Say what now? You want to leave the island altogether? That's a lot all at once."

"Didn't you like leaving Murphy and starting fresh?"

"Sure . . . but I didn't move off the island until after high school. It's not like a new place fixes everything. I didn't have any game on Murphy, I still didn't in Lincoln. I was a short guy who couldn't sit still in both places. The schools are the same too."

"I bet they don't have a loom or a kiln at Lincoln Bay. I bet their principal doesn't get everyone to try to cleanse their auras on Monday mornings."

"Maybe think about staying at Murphy School. It would make Mom happy," Carlos said. He didn't get it. "Let's get you back. It's a school night."

"I asked her to send the form yesterday. I want to go to Lincoln Bay." I could change my mind and stay at Murphy School—it wasn't like they ran out of space—but if I wanted to go to Lincoln Bay, we had to register before summer.

"How's it going with the dreams?" Carlos asked. I shrugged. "Fig. You're going to be okay." I didn't know if he meant with the dreams or middle school, but I nodded.

I thought Carlos would stop so I could hop out, but he paid the toll and drove up the ramp onto the boat. He wanted to surprise our parents for dinner. He dropped me off at the

Murphy dock to pick up the Rooster. That's what I started calling the truck, because of the painting on the side. He shook his head.

"If you get pulled over, I'll keep rolling like I don't even know you."

I ignored him and climbed up into the Rooster. I closed my eyes and got ready to look at the bear. I could feel it behind me, as if it had been waiting in the truck the way Chuck waits for us on the porch when we all go out. The bear smelled damp, like a mildewy towel. I turned and looked at it hard, but the fear didn't come. I exhaled. The longer I stared, the less it reminded me of the other bear and the more I remembered it was just a log.

I told the bear about wanting to move. He didn't talk back, obviously, but I felt better saying it out loud. Carlos blocked my way out of the parking lot and pointed until I turned on the Rooster's headlights. I followed him home, trying extra hard not to go over the yellow lines in case he was watching me in the mirror. After we got home, my brother came around to get a better look inside the truck.

"Whoa, Pops gave you *that*?" He pointed at the bear and climbed in for a closer look.

"No, I found it on the beach."

"And brought it home? Why? Isn't it heavy?" He gave it a little twist to test the weight.

"A friend helped. I'm going to find the owner and get rid of it. I can't believe I found a bear."

"Maybe you got the bear mojo or something. Sometimes stuff sticks. Like getting struck by lightning more than once. This isn't so bad."

"I guess," I said, because he was starting to sound like a Murpher again, even though he's been gone for years.

"That looks like a wishbone." He pointed at the Y the bear held. "Can I make a wish?"

I rolled my eyes so hard it hurt. No way would I tell him about Ethan.

"What do you need a wish for?"

"What does anybody need a wish for? To fix my problems."

"You don't have any problems," I said. "You want to wish for that girl from the coffee shop to talk to you? Or for the B's to win a game?"

"I don't want to worry about money anymore." He loves his job as an ecologist, but he doesn't get paid much to save the planet. Carlos cleared his throat. "I wish for a big fat raise so that I can buy even more apple fritters for my growing baby brother." He said it in an extra-deep, dramatic voice. He rubbed the bear's head, winked at me, and laughed. "Let's go eat."

Usually dinner is Mom, Leti, and me. Sometimes my dad is there, but mostly he's at work. It's hardly ever all of us anymore, but it was that night. Mom was talking to one of her sisters on the phone, but she hung up to hug Carlos.

Carlos set the table and asked about the festival.

"I'm not doing it this year," I said.

"Why not?"

"I guess I grew out of it," I said. Dad squeezed Mom's shoulder.

"How about you, Vivi?" Dad said. "You guys should do the singing human pyramid again. Musky was just talking about it yesterday at the lake." Musky is one of Dad's comrades. His real name is Paul, but Dad and the rest of the comrades call him Musky. I don't know why.

"Yeah, right," she said. "My human pyramid days are behind me."

"I've got a new pen pal through school," Leti told Carlos. "She lives in Scotland. They call elementary school primary school. And she's not in third grade. They call it year four."

"Tell him what they eat for snacks," I said.

"Potato chips are crisps, and cookies are biscuits! Pen pals are awesome," Leti said, and skipped back upstairs to finish her letter.

Dad offered to take us to the lake to stake out Marvelo. Carlos and Leti went, but I stayed home and cleaned the kitchen.

Mom made goat cheese, even though we have about a million logs of it in the freezer already.

"This is for Brenda and Musky," she said when she saw me looking. "I told them I would stop by tomorrow and install new window screens before it gets too hot. They've been getting butterflies in the house."

"Screens *and* cheese?"

Instead of answering, she told me how her family came north. I scrubbed the lasagna pan. My tía Felipa says they came over the border from Oaxaca in my Grandpa Armand's old Ford, because he had a job waiting at a silver mine in New Mexico. But Mom says Felipa's memory is bad, and butterflies carried her over the desert border. The rest of the family rode in the sweaty old car with squeaky doors. Mom and her cat, Bigote, got a ride from wild yellow butterflies on the big blue sarape she still keeps on the chair in the corner of her bedroom. The butterflies noticed her squished between her brothers in the back seat. When my grandpa stopped for a break, the other kids played chase, but Mom ate melon on the sarape with Bigote. The butterflies came down from the trees and worked together to lift the sarape up.

"How many?" I asked, like I did the first time she told me. She shuffled around the kitchen in slow motion, like she was running out of energy before she could finish the day.

"A lot. A herd of butterflies," she said.

"I don't know if you call them a herd."

"A flock? That doesn't sound right. A group of crows is called a murder." She hung balls of cheese wrapped in cloth on a rack over the sink.

"I don't think it's a murder either," I said. She could say the butterflies sang, or twirled through clouds, or something else to put the wink in the story and let me know she's messing with me, but she doesn't. She said the butterflies were just heading the same way as the Jaramillo family.

"Why would tía say you rode in the car?" I used to like Mom's stories, but when I was stuck in bed after the attack, I heard this one twice. She sat by my bed and talked more than she had her whole life. She retold stories about the island history—mermaids, greenhouses full of every kind of fruit you could think of, zebra cart races, and everything else. She told me what was happening around the island while I was stuck in bed—what the tamarin monkeys stole out of the community garden, the new wallaby babies riding in their moms' pouches, and how many parrots were in the tree outside my window. She made up conversations for them. She told me about the time she tried to climb aerial silks for the festival and got tangled up so much, she needed help right in the middle of her act. People still gave her a standing ovation. She didn't say it, but she was a star.

"Did you visit your abuela today?"

"She wasn't home," I said. "Carlos drove me by Lincoln Bay Middle. Did you send my registration papers?" She closed the pantry door.

"I filled them out, but I couldn't find a stamp. I'll mail them in the morning," she said. I cracked my knuckles and took two deep breaths.

"What if I went to stay with abuela for a while like Carlos did? I'll be going to Lincoln Bay next year anyway. It would be easier." My grandma lived about a mile from the school. I could probably walk.

"Carlos was going to college. You're twelve. Thirteen," she said. I loaded plates into the dishwasher from biggest to smallest, the way she likes. "I thought you were still considering staying at Murphy School. You could keep working on the garden, and Vera Swackhammer is probably the best algebra teacher in the state."

"I want to go to Lincoln Bay. And I want to live on the mainland. I never have bad dreams when I sleep at abuela's," I said. Mom frowned.

"You don't sleep there that often." She shook her head. She spent longer thinking about the butterfly story than she would about letting me move. "No. It's bad enough if you're on the mainland every day for school."

"I don't want to be on the island anymore," I said, and her eyes got wide. She held on to the counter and watched me. I crossed my arms.

"You're not old enough to make all your own choices, Newt. We would never see you if you lived in Lincoln," she said. "The answer is no." I turned the water off and left. Then I slammed my bedroom door and paced until the bunched muscles under my scar cramped.

Since Mom works on the island and her side of the family is in California, she doesn't leave Murphy much. We haven't been to California since I was in third grade, because it's expensive, even to drive, and it's a lot to ask for someone to watch Chuck and the animals. She's never really seen eye to eye with my grandma here—Dad's mom—so she visits only on special occasions. Dad runs errands after work in Lincoln to pick up medicine, the tortillas we like from the bodega on Spring Street, or noodles and fish sauce from Saigon Market. He doesn't ever complain. I asked him if we could do anything to help Mom and abuela get along. He said if he knew how to stop people from bugging each other, he'd be rich and wouldn't have to come home on the last ferry every night with an aching back, covered in plaster and paint.

I found cardboard boxes in the garage and packed books and games I could take to my grandma's house, where nobody made up silly stories about butterflies or believed in magic bears. I packed old toys and comics to give away. If the island was a box I could close the flaps and tape it up with all the bad memories inside, I would do it.

I heard Dad's truck pull up and Carlos's car leave. Mom and Dad wouldn't have to take care of me if I was in Lincoln. I could see Carlos and my cousins more often. My grandma always smiles as soon as she sees me.

I wrote my name and what was inside on the boxes. I moved them into the hallway, where my parents would see, but Little Leti came upstairs first.

"What are you doing?" she said.

"Packing stuff."

"Why?" She shuffled through the comics across the floor to sit on my bed. I picked the whole pile up and dropped them into a new box.

"I want to stay with abuela for a while. But Mom won't let me. Yet." I watched to see if she felt sad or mad or surprised or anything, but she kept her face blank. I talked fast. "I'll come back and visit. Or maybe you can come too? You'll be at Lincoln Bay in a couple of years. They have a real basketball team. You could be a Bulldog."

"Not even! Somebody will start a team on Murphy eventually. I'm going to live here forever," Leti said. "You can't leave. I would miss you too much." She looked at the pictures on the corkboard over my desk: our cousin Gabi's quinceañera,

Ethan and me digging around in the cove, our friend Rocket in the hot springs, and a fishing trip with my uncles in the mountains.

"Everybody leaves sometime, Let. I'll still visit. We can have Mastermind tournaments." I thought Leti was looking at my old Scrapper Pang drawing, but she reached out for the cat ears Mom wore the year she and Gilda did a Marvelo and Manxadon fight scene to surprise Dad. Fireworks blasted when Manxadon threw the bad guy through a wall. Leti wasn't born yet, but Mom warned me about the boom so I wouldn't be scared.

"I'm going to the festival with Abby and Ramona, and then we'll sleep over Ramona's house. It's going to be amazing." She read the program from the year Ethan and I did the card trick. He almost pushed me into the orchestra pit, but it was still great. "Can I have your room if you leave? Yours has a better view. And I could write letters here." She ran her fingers over the desk and looked out toward the pasture. I had Carlos's old desk, bed, and dresser. Dad brought them from our tío Ed's when he got a new set. Next they could be Leti's, I guess. "Someone else will have to take care of the goats, though. I'm not doing it."

She wouldn't look at me as she left, but her face was blotchy like before she cried. I curled up on the bed. If I could hibernate until fall, when everything would be different, I would.

CHAPTER 8

My dream changed after I told Carlos about it. It was the same, but slowed down and thick, like my brain needed to color in all the spaces in my memory. Sometimes afterward it feels like everything that's already bad is worse. A cool breeze makes my teeth chatter. Noises are extra loud. I can't hide when I've had a bad night. Dad says he can tell from my eyes. He offered me a ride to school and even stopped for cocoa.

I could barely stay awake. Grouchy teachers. Scratchy shirt. I didn't really fit in before, but I especially didn't now. This kid Stilton, who is named after moldy cheese and wears the same clothes all week, has more friends than I do. He's staying at Murphy School, of course. It's like I'm missing something everybody else has. Maybe it's because I'm quiet.

Or I'm one of the oldest kids in our grade. Or there's something I don't know, like I have the worst breath in the world. I've got Ethan and a few other friends. There's Rocket. He goes surfing a lot. His mom taught him how, and now sometimes he gets to school with wet hair and blue lips. He's probably going to Lincoln Bay. We used to be close, but he didn't visit after the attack, and we don't hang out much anymore. Maybe next year.

People assume that if you're on an island, you find ways to be friends with all the other kids, since you're the only ones there. But that doesn't happen, at least not on Murphy, and not for me.

I sit out gym class when my leg hurts. We're supposed to wear gym shorts, but I don't. Mom made a deal with Principal Erica for me to have a "lenient year." If I skip gym, I can go to the library, the art cottage, or the school garden. On Wednesday, I chose the garden. I wanted to be alone, but Rocket was there. He gets special permission to plant things three afternoons a week. He says it helps him think more clearly in class.

"How're the kittens?" I asked him. Rocket's cat had kittens a few days before. I put on some gloves and grabbed one of the hand rakes.

"They're so cute, dude. Three tiny little calico puffs and one gray one. Their mom put them behind the couch, so I laid out an old blanket and made it cozy for them. Mostly they sleep."

I scraped the weeds around some new tomato plants. They were still scrawny, but last year the school grew and donated over sixty pounds of tomatoes to the community food bank. Kids like Rocket volunteered to take care of the garden over the summer. They grew all kinds of stuff. No kid leaves Murphy without knowing how to compost and fertilize. I'd bet a hundred dollars there isn't a garden at Lincoln Bay.

"Did you decide about school next year?" I said.

"I don't know. I think Lincoln Bay would be cool, but I want to build boats." The older grades at Murphy build big wooden boats. "But you know the school on Palatine Island sounds pretty great too. Their science teacher is a real marine biologist, and the waves are stellar down there."

"Oh." Palatine Island is twenty miles south. We wouldn't be friends in Lincoln.

"You?"

I snagged a couple of peapods off a vine and munched.

"Lincoln Bay. My mom wants me to stay on Murphy, but my brother went. I'm thinking of moving there—my grandma lives near the school."

Rocket stopped patting compost around little corn sprouts.

"What about Ethan?" he said.

"What about Ethan?"

"Well, he's staying. Isn't he? I just thought you guys would stick together."

"You don't have to be in the same place to be friends," I said. "My mom sent the registration papers yesterday. I haven't told Ethan for sure yet, so don't say anything." It came out more defensive than I meant. Rocket dug his fingers straight into the dirt, no gloves.

"Being in the same spot definitely makes friendship easier." Rocket worked the dirt in new beds and I picked peas until the last bell rang.

I woke up on Sunday morning on the floor next to my bed in my sleeping bag. The bear's teeth cut into my calf. I've tried sleeping in every room in the house, but it finds me wherever I go. I tried to think of a new ending to the dream. Carlos said the wilder the better. I could poke the bear with a pin before he bit me and watch him pop into confetti. I pictured my body disappearing before the bite, teleportation-style, and I tried to see myself punching it in the nose. None of it cut through the brambles of the dream. Parrots squawked in the tree outside my window, and I couldn't go back to sleep. The sky wasn't even pink yet. I lay there shaking in a sweaty hand-me-down T-shirt. I wanted to get as far away from the dream as I could.

I took one of the books Leti gave me and grabbed apples from the kitchen for the goats. They aren't supposed to have much apple because of the sugar, but they love treats. If I moved to Lincoln, I would visit them on the weekends and sneak them new fruits to sample.

Once the sun was up, I went back inside to get ready to visit my grandma with Leti. The chickens followed me back to the house, but they don't try to come inside like the goats do. Mom tapped her nails on the counter while she waited for toast.

"Do you miss going to church?" I asked. She could go back to Lincoln more. There are pictures on our bookshelves from her First Communion and church potlucks. But she shook her head.

"Not really. I went my whole life, and the pews are hard."

"You could go with Beth and Ethan. They like their church. Or you could start a church here," I said, "with softer seats." I've never seen a woman in priest clothes, so maybe they'd wear something different. Mom would need a microphone. I smiled to show her it was a joke, but she looked confused.

"For me, making something with my hands is like a prayer. Listening to the birds from the porch is like a gospel."

"But not abuela's kind," I said. She readjusted the ribbon of milagros around her neck. Lately, she's been wearing a truck for the Rooster.

"No, not abuela's kind. Tell them hi for me, and I'm sorry I couldn't get off work." Mom gave me ferry money and went outside. I watched her carry a coil of wire like a truck tire out to the garage and close the door behind her. Dad would pick us up in Lincoln after his shift.

When Leti and I drove to the dock, I saw Izzy heading toward the spring pools with a woman in a big floppy hat. I waved and Izzy looked excited to see me, but we had to get to the ferry before it left. It was the end of the weekend, so a lot of tourists headed back from vacation houses and golf resorts on the other islands.

Once we were on the ferry, I picked out some chips from the concession stand, and Little Leti got a pretzel. We sat in a booth near the front, starboard side. *Starboard* is boat talk for the right side, but it's my favorite because it sounds like a spaceship headed far away.

People watched the water, read books, and tried to get service on their phones. A gray-haired couple kissed in the corner. No one looked around at the other passengers, except for one guy. A man by the pinball machine on the portside caught my eye over his coffee cup. He wore red pants and a mustard-colored velvet jacket. His hair reminded me of how my grandpa and uncles used to wear theirs back in the day, combed up and slick. A pompadour, it's called. I stared and the man stared back. He nodded at me without smiling. I made Leti move to a booth in the stern. She's not a baby anymore, so keeping an eye on her should be easy. Once I moved to Lincoln, Mom and Dad would have to trust her to be alone more instead of having me babysit. I went to the bathroom for two minutes to put some pain ointment on my knee and fill up my water bottle, and when I came back, she was telling the guy in the mustard jacket that I'm a good driver.

"Go-karts, she means," I said. Leti wanted to argue, but I squeezed her arm. His jacket was made from material like my tía Carrie's curtains. His boots used to slither. But it wasn't just the clothes. He looked like he didn't believe me about the go-karts and he wanted to say something about it. Instead, he asked where the stairs to the car deck were and left. I let out a long breath when he moved down the aisle. Leti read a comic.

"Don't talk to strangers, Leti! Especially not about our business."

"Everybody is a stranger at first," she said, and turned the page of her book without looking at me.

"Well, don't talk to strange strangers," I said. She twisted her face. I couldn't stay mad at her, because we were on our way to my grandma's house and it was going to be great.

—

"Slow down! These shoes are hard to walk in," Leti said. We headed down the ramp off the ferry. She stopped and adjusted one of the many straps on her sandal.

"Why didn't you wear your tennis shoes?" I said.

"Abuela likes it when we look nice." I looked at her closer. She wasn't wearing her usual T-shirt and track pants. She had on a skirt and a button-down blouse her nina sent for her last birthday. I was going to say she looked nice in her regular clothes, but I knew what she meant. I was wearing the new hoodie Carlos gave me and my best jeans. A noisy engine revved behind us, and I pulled Leti closer to me. The guy in the mustard jacket nodded as he passed in a purple van. It said MINERVA ANTIQUES & ODDITIES on the side, with a picture of an owl with butterfly wings. He revved the engine again. Leti barely noticed. She was looking for our dad. He waved from his truck with an arm covered in drywall dust.

"Vámonos, I want to shower and change at Carlos's before we go." When Dad comes home early some nights, he has to work extra on the weekends. The purple van passed, and we buckled up.

Carlos had an announcement, but he wanted to wait until we got to our grandma's.

"Go pick up some pan dulce to take to abuela's while I get cleaned up." Dad slid me a twenty, which goes a long way in our favorite panadería. Carlos says he picked his apartment to be close to the panadería. I believe him, because he loves that stuff. You can smell pan baking from his balcony. Plus, his apartment isn't far from our grandma, and he loves her too. We make it to Sunday dinner about once a month, but Carlos is there almost every week. I could be there every day when I moved.

I volunteered to carry the sweet bread to my grandma's. The bag gets greasy, but it's the best smell in the world, warm sugar and toasted flour.

We found abuela making tortillas, and Carlos clapped his hands to get everyone's attention.

"¡Gente, tengo buenas noticias! I got my first promotion at work—I'll get a raise and be in charge of some new programming!" Everybody cheered and patted his back. I laughed.

"That's just what you wished for!" I said, but the kitchen was too loud with all the "¡Felicidades!" and no one heard me. I grabbed an oreja and put the pan dulce in the big yellow bread box my grandma keeps filled on the table.

My grandma passed her plate to tía Leti so she could hug me again.

"How's your mom, mijo?" She smelled like rose perfume and masa.

"She's sorry she couldn't come, tía. She had to work. She said to say hi."

"Take a break, Mama, I got this," tía Leti said. "Newt,

did you get everything you wanted for your birthday?" I did a more-or-less thing with my hand, and she laughed at me. "Pobrecito, what do you need?"

My grandma watched from her chair. I didn't want to tell them about the truck, because she would get mad at Dad. It was an island thing. I should've just said it was fine.

"I kind of wanted a bike, but I didn't get one this year." Tía Leti ruffled my hair and laughed again, and my grandma smiled.

"Maybe we can look for one next time you come over," abuela said.

"Our old bikes are in the garage," tía Leti said, but abuela looked at me hard.

"He wants his own. A new one." She squeezed my hand. She sees me. "If you have a bike, you can ride over from Lincoln Bay and have lunch with me, if you don't mind leaving all your friends once in a while." It would have been the perfect time to ask her if I could live with her in Lincoln. She would understand. With all my cousins around, I wouldn't really be a new kid. I took a big breath and opened my mouth just as more cousins spilled into the kitchen.

"Newt! I didn't know you guys were here. ¿Qué onda?" My cousin Javi stood in the doorway in his puffer jacket and baseball hat. He's two years older. He tried to teach me to skateboard before the attack, but he doesn't talk about it any-more.

"Hey, Javi. Just waiting for summer, you know." Dad snuck in and tried to snag a tortilla, but tía Leti smacked his hand.

"And then middle school. ¡Órale! You gonna be a Bulldog or what?" Javi asked. He was at Lincoln Bay, but he'd be at the high school next year.

"That's right," I said, but Dad frowned.

"We'll see," he said. Everybody looked at me.

"Yeah, we will," I said.

CHAPTER 9

Before school on Monday, Ethan told me that he'd called the cryptozoology club in Portland to find out what proof we would need for Marvelo. I rolled my eyes, but he couldn't see it. His face was hidden behind a giant tuba case. He plays a new instrument every year. Last year was cello, but this year he wanted something shinier.

"They added another thousand dollars to the reward," he said. "I guess your dad called them too." Dad spent most of his free time now at Gertrude Lake, sometimes with his comrades but mostly alone. I never know if he's working late or monster stalking. We'd get kooky monster-hunting tourists again if he kept it up.

"Let's stake out the lake tonight after dark," Ethan said.

"What?" I walked out of the main building to the fortune-teller's cottage for math class and hoped he'd head to music class in the conservatory. It's the only school building that's used for the same thing as it was during the resort days. It's got nice acoustics, but I bet they didn't have a theremin or a hydraulophone back then.

"We can take the truck. We'll park nearby in case we need to run back in a hurry," he said.

"I'm getting low on gas," I said. It wasn't true, but the lake isn't far from where I got bit.

"I don't have any money," Ethan said, "but I'll give you twenty Murphy bucks."

The Murphy Council made its own money for a while when we were in kindergarten. It was money only for the island. Nobody got used to it. Murphy eventually went back to the regular green dollars, but everybody agreed that the island dollars were prettier. My parents still have some in a box in the dining room, in case it ever makes a comeback. Ethan collects it too.

"New shirt? I like it," I said. Ethan was wearing a red T-shirt with a T. rex carrying a stack of books.

"Thanks. My mom let me get it at the church rummage sale. I got a fishing pole too, so we can do that this summer. They had a metal detector too! Can you imagine? But it was fifty bucks." If I'm ever rich, I'm going to buy Ethan a metal detector. We sat down and Ethan leaned in to whisper: "If we see Marvelo, you have to sign up for the festival and we can figure out an act."

"If we don't see Marvelo, you can't talk about him or the festival anymore," I said. He argued, but the morning announcements started.

Ethan wouldn't look at me when Principal Erica started her list: Kids going to Lincoln Bay had to register for their ferry pass card for fall. School ended in three weeks, and the barbecue and field day would be in the cove as usual. The older kids would show off and race the boats they'd built.

My stomach flopped when I looked at Ethan. I would need to tell him about moving. If Leti or Rocket said something before I did, he'd be even madder than he already was about Lincoln Bay. I told myself I would tell him later so I wouldn't interrupt the announcements: Everyone was welcome to come help paint the new mural at the People's Pub. Lyric almost jumped out of his seat with excitement. The kindergarten class's gerbil escaped overnight, and the school garden needed weeding. I'd tell him after they found the gerbil.

After school, Ethan came over with Boxwood while I made quesadillas for Leti and me. Mom and Dad were both at work.

"My mom says it's cool if we go to the lake, but only if we

have an adult with us," he said, and helped himself to a plum from the bowl on the table.

I called my dad. It rang and rang. I was about to tell Ethan we were out of luck, but Dad picked up right before it went to voice mail.

"Newt, everything okay?" I took a deep breath and asked if maybe he could come with us to the lake if he wasn't busy. He said yes so fast it was hard to understand him.

"The best vantage point is probably the north side of the lake," he said. "If he comes up where I saw him last time, we'll see the whole thing." He went on about people who supposedly saw Marvelo at night a long time ago, and I pressed a drip pattern in the doorframe paint with my thumbnail.

"All right. Ethan's coming too."

"Órale, I've got a good feeling about this! I'll be off in an hour. See you soon." Ethan called his mom, and I made him a quesadilla even though he had already eaten chicken teriyaki at his house.

Dad called back and said he had to work late. Again. It would be safer if we waited and went together. I listened and watched Ethan and Boxwood split the quesadilla.

"Oh well," I said, and tried to look disappointed.

Ethan said, "My mom already thinks your dad is going to be there, and your dad knows we're going. Think of what we could do with the reward money." There was zero chance of getting that money, but I nodded. Mom got home from work, and I told her we were going out. Once I told Ethan about moving off the island, he'd probably be too mad to hang out with me anymore. It made my chest ache, so I tried not to think about it.

"You guys don't want to stay and watch basketball with us?" Leti told Ethan about player stats, and Mom sewed black fabric. We left. The goats crowded around the gate and bleated at us when we passed, like they wanted to go for an evening stroll.

It was my first time driving in the dark. I tried to take down the fuzzy dice so I could see a little better, but the knot was tight. Ethan talked the whole time about the tricks he'd been training Boxwood to do. He could make him bark on command. I drove extra slowly and kept an eye out for deer. Most locals avoided the north side of the lake, because it's boggy and smells gross. We sat on a muddy bank under cedars, not too far from the path. Boxwood waited in the truck with a rawhide. I'd brought my grandma's chocolate zucchini bread, but the mud was too smelly to eat anything.

"I showered with the unscented goat soap from your mom," Ethan said, "so in case Marvelo came out, he couldn't smell me. Mr. Roush said komodo dragons can smell people from over a mile away. Maybe Marvelo has a good sense of smell too." Path lights shone behind us. The lights from the café and pizza parlor sparkled across the lake, but brambles and brush kept it dark around us. Two guys sat in camp chairs on the far shore in front of the dark theater.

"Now you smell like kid instead of soap," I said. "Maybe he wants kid for dinner." I slapped a mosquito and looked back toward the Rooster. We could make a wish on the statue not to see a real bear, but a lake monster was all the magical stuff I could take for one night.

I pointed my flashlight in the shallows. Red-, yellow-, and blue-striped cichlids darted through the light beam like they were onstage. When I was little, Mom and Gilda had a festival act where they were cichlids swimming through hoops under blue lights. I tried to tell Ethan it was funny that the fish reminded me of people that were fish, but he just told me to put my flashlight away. We waited and nothing monsterly happened. My butt got cold. Fog rose on the water. Frogs and night birds made most of the sounds.

I started to tell him about moving, but I couldn't. If he gave me a look like Leti did, I might cry right there on the boggy side of the lake.

"What if you went to Lincoln Bay next year too?" I said.

"It's too late to register."

"No, it's not. My mom just sent my registration a couple of days ago. She said I can still go to Murphy School if I change my mind."

"I don't want to. I don't know anybody there." The fog thickened until we couldn't see the other side of the lake.

"You'd know me. And there are other kids we know going too." I said. Ethan slurped tea straight out of a thermos.

"I wouldn't fit in. Kids in Lincoln have more money. Elijah told me he got teased for having holes in his pants." Elijah was at Murphy last year before he transferred. Ethan took a deep breath and blew it all out until he looked deflated. "Besides, I'd get back too late to volunteer at the museum. And there's Marvelo, and now you have a statue that grants wishes. Why would anyone want to leave?" His eyes glittered in the dark. It was no use arguing.

I'm too embarrassed to tell Ethan, but Mom said she saw Marvelo once too. When I was a baby, she took me out in the swan paddleboat one night to see a meteor shower. She swears he came up and glided past the boat, scraping silver scales along the side. Or they might have only looked silver in the moonlight, which shone too bright to see any meteors. She says that we stayed out for hours. She paddled back only after I got fussy and cried, so I wouldn't wake up the people in the lake cottages. He didn't come back again that night, and it was probably my fault for making such a racket. That's how the story goes.

We sat in silence. I left the flashlight off, except when the leaves rustled behind us and I had to check for bears. I scooted away from the thicket and massaged my knee, just in case we had to run.

"I'm glad there's still a chance you could stay at Murphy School," Ethan said, and I knew I couldn't tell him about moving yet.

"I met somebody. A girl," I said.

"Where?"

"On the beach. She's visiting."

"You like her?"

"She's interesting." The reflections from the path lights turned the water into a liquid galaxy.

"How?"

"I don't know. She knows . . . science."

"She sounds like something you made up. Like one of your goats got lost on the beach and you imagined it was a girl." He laughed into his hand.

"She was there when I went back for the bear," I said.

"You didn't tell her about the bear granting wishes, did you?" Ethan asked. "Maybe we shouldn't tell too many people until we figure out what's going on." I said I wouldn't tell, which was easy, since there was nothing to tell.

Even when the mud seeped through our pants and mosquitos bit us, Ethan wanted to stay. A small raccoon passed by, and my heart skipped. People say that, but it doesn't feel like a skip. It feels like it could run right out of your body if your ribs weren't making a cage. Ethan raised his eyebrows and made a yikes face like the raccoon scared him too, but it didn't. Ethan isn't scared of spooky stuff. He was just trying to make me feel better. He's the best friend I ever had.

I heard the rumors about what was in his backyard before we became friends. The first few times I went over to his house, Ethan kept the curtains facing the backyard closed. When I got there the third time, he walked straight through the house out the back door. All of it was true. The part of the backyard that wasn't lawn or vegetable garden was one big animal cemetery.

"Go ahead, look around. I mean, if you want to," he said. I wasn't sure if I wanted to or not, but I walked around, in case he'd feel bad if I didn't. "It's a spiritual thing. The pope says animals go to heaven." He said it like I might fight about it. "But it's not just that. My mom learned about different kinds of burials in college, and it stuck with her." I tried to think of something to say that wasn't rude.

"Is this because of your dad?" is what I said then, but I would take it back now. Ethan looked like he could have hit me, but he pushed the anger somewhere else.

"No. We spread his ashes in Joshua Tree National Park.

This cemetery's only animals. It's been back here since I was little. My dad built the first few pyramids."

"Do you, um, mummify them first?" I asked.

"What? No!" Ethan laughed. "A few got cremated, but most are buried."

When his parents told their friends about it, other Murphers asked if they could do it too, so not all the graves came from Ethan's family. It was a relief, because there are a lot of graves and grave-type things back there. It's a big yard. It turns out his mom sold space when they needed money, and it turned into a thing. A Murphy Thing.

There are enough different kinds of animals back there to make a dead-animal zoo. The biggest are the deer crypts. Driftwood antlers and plastic fruit hang over their doors. Gravestones and pyramids made from everything from rocks and bricks to driftwood and ceramic figurines stand in bizarre rows. A line of tiny crystal pyramids runs along the back fence. Ethan explained that those belonged mostly to hamsters and mice. Some were pets, and some of them their former cat, Mr. Crinkles, caught in the garage. The smallest pyramid in the yard, at the end of the line, is Mr. Crinkles's, the size of a chocolate kiss. Beth said he deserved no bigger monument than his tiny rodent victims.

—

Boxwood whined in the truck, and I wondered if it freaked him out to go to their backyard. But before I could ask Ethan, I heard something else.

"*Shhh,*" he said. Something moved through the water in the fog, not far away. Ethan sat up and held a finger to his lips. I pulled branches back. Something splashed, and a murmuring buzz came toward us. Ethan and I sat frozen. I wanted to fold up and hide, or run back to the truck. I squinted but couldn't see anything. A couple of bats hunted bugs through the fog. A small ripple of wake lapped against the bank, and we both jumped. The wake grew. I heard something that sounded like crying, and my stomach knotted up.

I was too young when Mom told me about La Llorona. Something had cried outside in the yard, and I asked if it was a cat.

"Maybe," Mom said. "Or it could be La Llorona."

"Who's that?" I said, like a dummy.

"La Llorona," Mom said, "is a ghost lady who walks by the water, looking for her lost children. She drowns any kids she finds."

It freaked me out bad. I pictured La Llorona walking loops all night around the beaches. Sometimes the wind howls during storms, and it sounds like La Llorona wailing. I told my parents once, and they looked out the kitchen window and said they could see her coming. I know they were joking, but still, I never go to the beach at night. But there we were.

"Ethan, let's get out of here."

We crept backward through the mud to the path under the rainbow canopy of lights. The brush and trees muffled the mysterious sounds and hid us from the water.

"You know, these lights emit special rays to repel lake monsters," Ethan said. "They're designed specifically as a monster-free path through the park. It's one hundred percent safe for humans, but it repels anything that's recently crawled up from the depths." One side of his face glowed pink, and the other green.

"My dad said Herb hung them up to make it look like a supernova. He didn't say anything about monster safety." It's supposed to be like outer space. Herb owns the market, but he runs an astronomy club too. He put two hundred strings of lights between the trees over the path at first, but Murphers have been adding more for years.

"Well, yeah. It's a supernova safety portal. If you manage to somehow get to thirty miles per hour when you get to the bottom of the hill, you'll be transported."

"Uh-huh. To where?"

"How would I know? I'm way too slow," Ethan said, and I cracked up. It wasn't even funny, but he laughed and I laughed harder. We couldn't hear whatever was in the lake, and the lights made us multicolored. I could have stayed there forever.

"That was fun," Ethan said when we got to his house. He shut the door and walked up his driveway. I waited for him to get inside before I drove away, like my dad does.

The truck was too quiet without Ethan. I talked to the bear to fill the silence. "I have to call you something. I used to have a teddy bear named Huxley from my grandma, until puppy Chuck came along and used it as a chew toy. How about Huxley?" It fit, and of course, he didn't complain. Once I'd parked next to the house, I got in the back and kept talking. Maybe if I could get used to him, I could get used to real bears again. I talked about school, and what we used to do at the festival, and what I would do for my part of the tourist pamphlet. It made me feel better.

"Thanks for listening," I said. I crept into the house and got ready for bed. I closed the bathroom door so the light wouldn't wake up Leti. The floor creaked in the living room, and soft steps passed down the hallway. I turned the water off. I wanted to brag to someone that we hadn't seen anything at the lake. But when I came out of the bathroom, the house was dark and still.

CHAPTER 10

Ethan brought a box of his favorite old magazines about ghosts, UFOs, and angel sightings to school. Half the stories he tells are from those magazines. A family moved into a haunted house in Ohio, and no one saw them again. People at campsites in four states all saw the same pink lights floating around the moon one night. He loves that stuff.

Still, when Mr. Roush told us to pick lab partners, for real science, I wished Ethan was there, but he was in math class. We were building DNA chains in pairs, so Mr. Roush told us to "find someone with similar DNA." Kids with blond hair paired up, and a few went for eye color. Rocket has black hair like me, but he was late to school again. I watched everybody else race around until it was just Stilton and me.

"I don't think we have any DNA in common," Stilton said. He is tall and lean, with red hair and freckles. The only thing we share is less-than-ideal names. Half the kids at Lincoln Bay look like me, which is one of the top reasons I want to go.

"You're both human, gentlemen," Mr. Roush said. "You are more alike than different." He made each team roll our tongues, clasp our hands, and eat cilantro and raw kale to see if we thought they tasted gross. All of it is genetic. It could have been fun with someone else, but I ended up doing most of the writing while Stilton flicked a folded paper football at the wall.

At lunch, Ethan tried to do a chin-up on the ladder in our school cafeteria, which used to be the resort's indoor Olympic swimming pool. The older kids eat lunch in the deep end. Little Leti and her friends sit on the stairs in the shallow end. We sit toward the middle by the slant but not under the chandeliers. They've been there since the resort first opened, and Ethan thinks one of the dusty crystals will knock someone out if it falls. A ketchup packet has been caught in the middle chandelier for at least three years.

"We should get the band back together," Ethan said. He wasn't eating lunch, because his mom gave him fish stew. He wanted to trade for my burrito, but I said no.

"We've never had a band," I said.

"Yeah, but for the festival. I say we start a band. Let's do it." He pushed his bangs out of his eyes. He already looked like he could be in a band. He wore a holey shirt from a 5K run eight years ago that would look like a hand-me-down on anyone else but looked cool on him.

"I can't play any instruments," I said and chewed a dried apple ring.

"You're totally missing the point. I already have our name." He tried another chin-up.

"For a band?"

"Yes, Fig."

"Don't call me—"

"Fear of Grapes!" Ethan hopped off the ladder and raised his arms over his head like a victory. "Get it?"

"No." I put the rest of my rings back in my lunch bag for Margie, my favorite goat.

"Fear of Grapes because grapes have wrath. Like the book!" Mrs. Elum had passed out worn paperback copies the day before. Mom says there are better books for us to read, but she's not the teacher. "We could use your truck to haul gear for gigs." Ethan slapped the table like it was a bongo. He played at least five instruments, but not the obvious ones. I'm pretty sure we'd need guitar or drums for the band.

"I don't think that's what the book is about," I said.

"What do you want to do for the festival? We could juggle, or balance on stuff again, or rock out! I'm going to wish on the bear that you'll sign up today!" Ethan fake-whispered.

"People don't get wishes," I whispered back. Everything echoes in the pool like a giant bowl of noise.

"People get wishes all the time," he said as I picked up my bag. "I wished for frozen yogurt last night, and then I found some in the freezer." That's not the sort of wish I meant, and he knew it. Wanting a snack that's already in your freezer isn't the same as wishing for something big. Something you need. That kind of wishing can be a waste of time.

I folded my seat closed. It flopped down again, and I left it. Chairs at our table came from a couple of old theaters. They're the soft red velvet kind that you have to fold down before you sit. At the start of the year, the teachers brought in a giant antique chair just for me. They thought it would be easier to get in and out of, but it looked like a throne. My parents asked them to let me have a regular theater seat again. Ethan and Rocket had to help me out of it for a couple months.

"I'll see you later." I headed to the gallery for language arts.

On days when I drove to school, I parked three blocks away. Partly to have somewhere I definitely wouldn't need to reverse, and partly so nobody would see when I drove away after school. But today someone stood on the running board, peeking in the Rooster window.

"Newt! Is this your truck?" Lyric said. He wore a uniform shirt from a restaurant that we don't have on Murphy, paint-smudged cargo shorts, and laceless, graffitied sneakers. Pretty much what he wore every day.

"What are you doing? Get down!"

"Is this your truck, though? That's rad." He jumped off. We talk sometimes, and our dads are friends, but we don't hang out. Lyric ran his hand over the plume of the tail. "Cool rooster, bro. Listen, I heard you guys talking in the cafeteria. Don't get mad! I didn't mean to. Sound carries in the pool."

"Do you need a ride?"

"No, I want to see inside for a minute. You said something about a magic bear." I looked around for Ethan, but of course he wasn't there.

"I definitely didn't say I had a magic bear."

"But you and Ethan talked about a good luck bear or something."

"Not a real bear. It's a statue."

"Yeah, otherwise, I wouldn't have asked to get in the truck with it." Lyric glanced at my leg. "I figured you wouldn't keep a real bear." He looked back through the window. "Can I see it? I want to make a wish."

I stared at him. "I just want to go home, it's been a long day."

"Please. There's something I want." Lyric held his hands out, palms together, as if praying. "A lot."

"What is it?"

"Why should I tell you?"

"I don't want you to wish for anything bad. And it's my bear."

"So it's true?" Lyric's mouth hung open. I moved closer and leaned against the Rooster.

"It's just a coincidence."

"But maybe not?" Lyric raised his eyebrows. "I want to do the poster. That's all. I swear."

"What poster?"

"For the Marvelo Festival. You know, how there's a contest every year to design it and they hang it everywhere. Even on the mainland and other islands," he said. Any Murphy resident can submit a design. People kept the posters after the festival ended. Lyric obviously liked to paint and draw, but the competition was tough. "All the entries had to be submitted today. I'm taking mine down to the festival office in person as soon as it dries. They'll make copies of the winner and start hanging them this week."

"Are you sure that's what you want? More than anything?"

"Absolutely! I've never wanted anything more." He was a

ball of happy energy, sure that the poster would make everything perfect, and it made my chest ache. I used to get that excited about the festival. I opened the back doors and gestured toward Huxley's corner.

He looked at Huxley and back at me. "Do I have to say it out loud?"

"I'm not sure. Probably? It's not really going to work," I said. Lyric would wish to win the contest, it wouldn't happen, and I could show Ethan that the answer to your problems doesn't wash up on the beach.

Lyric inspected the bear for a full minute before squatting in front of it. I climbed through the back and sat in the driver's seat. Lyric scratched his leg, pulled the tongue out on his sneaker, and shifted around. I twirled the fuzzy dice and emptied my water bottle.

"I wish . . . they select my poster design and use it for this year's Marvelo Festival," Lyric said and nodded. "Can you think of anything else I should say?"

"Nope."

Lyric touched his palm to the bear's chest, maybe to where its heart would be, before hopping out. "Thanks, Newt." He walked away like everything was jake. I rolled down my window.

"Hey!" I called. "Don't tell anybody about this. It's, you know . . ."

"What?"

"Probably nothing to get excited about," I said.

"Or maybe this time next year, everybody will be wishing on your bear and you'll be the most popular guy on Murphy."

I groaned. "Don't tell, all right?"

Lyric waved and kept walking. I looked back at my wooden pet. Mom had Chuck and the goats. Ethan had Boxwood. I had Huxley.

Dad asked me to help Arlene, the librarian, after school. I brought Leti along so she could learn more about Morocco for another pen pal. Arlene sat at her desk and looked like she couldn't wait to find me a book.

"Newt! Did you drive your truck here?"

"It was not my idea, and I've been practicing a lot," I said.

Arlene waved her hand. "I've seen you around. I hoped Murphy might be getting a food truck, so that was a disappointment. But I'm glad you're here. Cookie?" She pointed to the snack cart she keeps by the water fountain. "I know you like chocolate chip."

"They're my favorite," I said. Her cookies looked like they were straight out of a commercial, perfectly round with just the right number of chips. She made a lot of different cookies and muffins, but these were the best. Classic.

"Take a couple. The trick is to salt them just before you put them in the oven." I stuffed one in my mouth and a handful in my pocket. She looked relieved. "My brother Randy is bringing over a few boxes of books on the ferry. Can you meet him at the dock? Randy can help you load."

"Okay, but what's your brother going to say about me driving the truck?"

"He won't ask. But if he does . . . you know . . ." She trailed off. "Let me get the dolly. And try to look older."

I nodded, like that was a thing I could do.

I drove to the ferry and parked by the dock, close enough to load the books but far enough not to get noticed. A guy who looked like Arlene but with a beard was stacking boxes on the landing. He saw me rolling the dolly down the planks and waved.

"Hi! Arlene told me you were coming."

"Are those all books?"

"Yeah, a lot, eh?" Randy pushed the dolly, and we arranged the boxes inside the truck. "This is your ride?"

He'd already seen me drive up, so I told the truth. "Birthday present."

"I see. Probably not your sixteenth birthday," Randy said.

"Probably not," I said. My neighbor George pedaled past on a cruiser bike with a spiked canopy, wearing nothing but flip-flops, swimming trunks, and a fuzzy motorcycle helmet.

"They sure like to keep things interesting around here, don't they?"

"Yup," I said. "They really do."

Randy shrugged and hopped inside the Rooster, like driving with me would be an adventure.

Back at the library, Arlene met us outside before I turned off the engine. While they unloaded the books, I watched the monkeys playing in the trees. Truman Murphy brought a couple from Bolivia, and now a whole troop stays mostly next to the library. It's their own little monkey bubble on the island. Cute little mustached faces watched me from the closest branch. Arlene might sneak them cookies.

I closed the back doors and crawled through to the driver's seat. I waved goodbye, but Arlene ran over and held out an envelope.

"It's not much, but I wanted to give you a little something for helping out," she said. A small stack of bills poked out under the flap.

"You already gave me cookies." I tried to push the envelope back, but she held her hands up.

"You did a job, Newt. You should get paid. It would have been difficult without your truck. It's not much, so I'm also going to wipe out any of your overdue fines." I looked at her. Scrapper Pang never took a payment when he saved a civilization, but I'm not an intergalactic superhero.

"Thanks, Arlene, but my parents will probably make me give it back anyway."

"Well, you don't have to tell them. You're getting pretty good at keeping secrets." She nodded toward the Rooster. I thanked her and left before she changed her mind.

CHAPTER 11

When I got home, I cleaned the goat pen, cuddled the babies, scrubbed out their trough, and basically did everything I could to avoid driving practice. This time, Mom went with me and gave some good tips, like checking blind spots and coasting between the gas and the brake to make the ride less lurchy. She put new seat covers in the truck, taped a piece of plywood over the holes in the floor, and put a rag rug on top. It made driving a lot quieter, and I wasn't distracted by the blurry road whooshing past my feet. She filled the gas tank too.

"Newton. Where did that come from?" I didn't even have to look to know she was talking about Huxley.

"I found it. I'm looking for the owner," I said. There hadn't been any bear claimers yet.

"It's a bear. Right?" She turned around and looked at it closer. "I saw the flyers in town, but I guess I should have looked at them closer. I don't understand."

"It's just a coincidence." I told her how we'd found it. "Maybe it's helping me not be afraid of bears anymore." I pulled up in front of the hardware store, and she hopped out to cover someone else's shift.

"If the owner doesn't show up, get rid of it. I don't like it," she said.

"Okay, Mom." I went back to Echo Beach, half hoping to see Izzy, or a good sunset. I saw both. I walked straight toward her under a pink sky, as if that was the plan all along.

"Hello," she said and eyed my goat-hair-covered shirt. Hair and dust covered my shorts too. I smelled like a goat. It's a good smell, like sweet grass, but I understand that other people don't like it as much as I do. I tried to stand downwind, but she was out of luck.

"I'm haunted by goats," I said.

"Ghosts?" Izzy's eyebrows went up.

"No . . . goats. My mom makes goat cheese and soap. She trades it with neighbors and sells some to a few restaurants. She works at the hardware store too. You've probably seen her if you needed lightbulbs. We have nine."

"Lightbulbs?"

"Goats. Their fur gets all over." I brushed at my shirt, but only a few strands floated away. Izzy tried to catch one and smiled.

"What are their names?"

"Margie, Liz, Greta, Isadora, Beauregard, Fozzy, Buster, Speckles, and Porridge. Fozzy, Speckles, and Greta are babies. Margie is my favorite. This is hers, probably." I brushed my shirt again.

"I think goats are pretty cute. Like, way better than sheep."

"Do you want to visit them?" I asked. "They're great, but they poop a lot."

Izzy nodded immediately. "You can't scare me," she said.

I laughed and looked away, but the air glowed all around us.

Izzy noticed it too. "Someday they'll find out that the glowing light that happens on days like this is because of a great microscopic bird migration," she said.

"What?"

"That's what makes the air between the dirt and the clouds seem healthy and rosy like baby cheeks," she said. "The only clue that the birds are there at all is the sun reflecting off their tiny feathered wings."

I squinted around our heads, as if I could spot one. Microscopic birds were more interesting than misty haze. "Maybe we should follow them when they leave. Wherever they go."

"We won't be able to see which way they're heading, so

we'll just stay in the light," Izzy said. "Or we can stay here and just appreciate that we're part of their migratory path." She faced the sun.

I didn't want her to see me staring at her, so I counted anemones on the rocks. They look like flowers, but if something touches them, they close up into slimy green donuts.

"We made some noodles with that the other day, and it tasted pretty good." Izzy pointed at wet green strips floating between the rocks.

I crinkled my nose. "Isn't that algae?"

"Seaweed *is* algae. We eat it all the time. There's sushi, obviously, but they add it to foods for nutrition too. That's sea lettuce, and it's tasty." She looked like she meant it, but it didn't make me want to try it. Izzy gasped. "Did you see that bird? I'm not kidding. A big one between the trees. It was such a bright green. It looked like a parrot!"

"It could be—a bunch live here, maybe a dozen?" I said. "They were part of an island zoo a long time ago. These are probably their grandbirds. It's more than one kind. If you see the whole flock, they have different colors and sizes. They steal goat food, and they love the cherries from the tree by my window."

"Oh yeah. My grandma told me about the aviary," Izzy said. Murphy Aviary had a ton of birds in the resort days.

Lots escaped, and some—mostly turacos, flamingos, and parrots—stayed on the island.

Izzy and I walked along the water toward the marina.

"They come really early to my house," I said. "It's usually still dark. And they make a ton of noise."

"Like 'Polly-want-a-cracker'?"

"No, screeches. They all screech at once. Each one is a sheet of metal grating over a pipe."

She laughed.

It's not funny at five a.m. when I haven't slept well.

"They freak out the squirrels that live in the attic pretty bad."

"You have squirrels in your attic?"

"Yeah, they're nocturnal. Only on Murphy Island. Nobody knows why."

Some kids would ask what *nocturnal* meant, or change the subject, but Izzy talked about other night creatures, like aye-ayes and bush rats. We passed the part of the beach where Ethan and I had found Huxley, but except for kelp and sticks, it was empty. I tried not to limp. I staggered a little but played it off like I was looking closer at a bright red brittle star in a tide pool.

"Maybe the parrots would talk if you taught them," she said. "Pet parrots can learn over a thousand words."

I asked her how she knew that, but she shrugged. "All

right," I said. "I'll train them. Next year you won't be able to cross the island without chatting with a dozen parrots."

She smiled and buried her feet in the sand. When Leti does that, I try to tip her over, but I left Izzy alone.

"I heard there was a bird act at the festival," she said. "Maybe somebody trained them."

"I doubt it. Will you be here for that? It's different, but it's usually fun."

"Maybe. I saw it once when I was little. My grandma told me so many stories about performers on the island." Izzy put shell bits into her sweatshirt pocket. "Want to meet here on Sunday? We could try to train a parrot. It's cool that they don't fly away from the island."

"I'm sure some do."

She frowned, and I wanted to make her smile again.

"Want to come over and feed the goats instead?"

"Yes," she said, and the whole world kept glowing.

The teachers had a meeting, so there was no school. Leti woke me up in the morning right after I dreamed that the bear jumped on me and I screamed. But I still couldn't sleep in.

"*Shhh,* Newt. It's just me." She patted my leg so gently, I could barely feel it. "Are you all right?"

"Yeah, sorry." I held my hand against my chest like it could calm down my heart.

"I've heard you before. Dreaming. I don't mean to, but it comes through the wall." Leti took a step closer. "Is it awful?"

"It's not so bad." I smiled at her. "Is Mom gone? Do you need something?"

"She's still here. Dad's on the phone for you. He wants you to help haul some kayaks to the cove, because Musky Barnes has a dead battery."

I rolled down the Rooster's windows so it could fill up with low-tide air and blow away the last of the dream feeling. As I drove to Musky's, I told Huxley all the gritty dream details. I tried making up some other endings, like Carlos said. I skipped breakfast, so in my newest version, the bramble vines turned to spaghetti and I ate my way out. I parked and Musky spotted the bear when I opened the back doors.

"Hey, I've seen that fella before. Whose is it?" He pushed a kayak into the truck. He takes tourists for zero-emission bird- and whale-watching trips around Murphy and nearby islands.

"I found it on the beach," I said. "Do you remember where you saw it?"

"Seems like someone used to keep it near the water. We passed it in the kayaks. I love bears." He shrugged, like he owed me an apology. He slid another kayak past the silver cupboards. Musky wasn't kidding about loving bears. He usually wore a bear suit to pass out candy on Halloween.

"Ethan thinks the bear can grant wishes." I rolled my eyes. I wanted Musky to laugh, but he squinted at Huxley.

"Because of the wishbone in his hand? Did he wish on it?"

"Yes." He pushed another kayak in and climbed up to the bear as quick as a rogue wave.

"I wish . . . I wish that I'd find my ring." He gave the bear's shoulders a squeeze and nodded. "Is that it, Newt?"

"I guess so," I said. He climbed back out of the truck. I moved some of my books and things to make more room for the kayaks. Everybody had a wish ready to blurt out. "You don't really believe that will help, do you?"

"You never know, right?" he said. "I've been looking everywhere for a month. Brenda is gonna kill me. I lost *the* ring. We had 'em made special for our wedding thirty-two years ago." Musky held up his bare left hand. He told me how he put it on a chain around his neck so it wouldn't get messed up while he sanded a chair. The clasp must have broken, because it was gone when he finished sanding.

"I hope you find it," I said. "But I'm not sure the bear will be any help."

"Let's look at the facts. . . . Maybe there's something funny about that bear. And it never hurts to hope."

I nodded, but neither of those were facts. Hoping I could live with my grandma wasn't getting me there. Hoping that I'd get a bike for my birthday hadn't worked. Neither did hoping that somebody on the island would act normal.

"Newt, before you split . . ." Musky trailed off. He rubbed his no-ring hands on his jeans. "Listen, your dad told me that you're still having a hard time from what happened last year. I don't know much about bear attacks, but I know about bad stuff." He didn't say what, but Musky fought in the war.

"I'm all right," I said.

He smiled and crammed three more kayaks on top of the others.

"No, you're not. And neither was I. I woke up screaming nearly every night after my third tour. I made some changes. We left San Diego and moved here. Brenda got the boats, and I started paddling. Started talking about it too."

It felt like there was a thread, like a strand of barely there spiderweb from him to me. It made it both better and worse that we were in the Bad Stuff Club. He'd been watching the trees while he talked, but now he looked right at me with sharp gray eyes.

"If you hold on to the fear, you'll never make it through. I served with guys who made it out but they've gone dark." I leaned back and the thread broke. My stomach ached.

"It's not the same," I said. "They enlisted. I never signed

up for . . . what happened. Thanks, though." He's a hero, and I'm the kid with scars.

"I know, but it can be better."

"People always ask if I'm okay," I said. "But I don't think I have the same kind of okay as them anymore. They just want me to say I'm good so they feel better."

"I know, Newt," he said. "Just remember—nobody's okay, and we're all okay." I could only take short breaths. He slapped the side of the truck. "Brenda will meet you at Fitz Beach and you can drop the kayaks there."

I could feel the tears coming, so I started the truck and got out of there as fast as I could.

CHAPTER 12

Lyric's poster won. At our school assembly, we learned that the judges chose his poster out of 183 entries. He was the first kid to win for as long as anybody remembered. His poster was good. I would never have known to put those colors together, but they looked great. He swung down the ladder at our table at lunch and gave me a special thank-you card with a sketch of Huxley.

"I'm going to tell everybody about your bear, Newt. That's amazing."

"Please don't," I said.

"People should know. You're going to be famous!"

"Lyric, don't say anything," I said.

Ethan leaned forward and said, "We're planning on revealing the bear at the Marvelo Festival. Promise not to say anything for the next couple weeks?" Lyric finally agreed and left for the art cottage.

"Ethan!" I kicked him under the table.

"Ow! That's another wish to come true! We can take the bear to the festival, and people can wish on it. You'll barely have to do *anything,* and we can still participate." He was a natural at the festival. He didn't need me there.

"I don't want to be in the festival! And there's nothing special about the bear. It's just coincidence." I got up and cleared off my lunch, even though I wasn't done.

"Sherlock Holmes said the universe is rarely lazy enough for coincidence," Ethan said. "Newt, what are you going to wish for? You have to do it before someone comes and takes it back."

"Sherlock wasn't real. Whatever you think the bear is, it isn't real either. It's stupid, and I'm tired of talking about it." I took the ladder instead of the stairs, even though it hurt my knee. I hoped Ethan would take the hint and leave me alone, but he followed.

"Sherlock was totally real!" Ethan said.

"He's made-up!"

"If anybody else's wish comes true, we sign up for the

festival. The deadline is this week. We'll take the bear, and people can wish."

"I have to concentrate on the brochure project." We went to the library. Mrs. Ribchester said I needed to pick a more specific topic by the end of the day. Tide pools was too broad, since a lot of kids were writing about specific plants and animals. Lyric and a couple of other kids would illustrate.

I waited for him to get a reference picture of a sea cucumber so I could use the computer. Tide pools are full of different creatures. I looked up microscopic gold, to check on Ethan's gold dust theory. Maybe someone on Murphy could invent a filter and we could all get rich. I didn't find anything on the gold, but there is a lot of microscopic life in tide pools. Enough to feed the barnacles and anemones and other filter feeders. There's even something called a water bear.

I froze when I saw it. I wanted to power down the computer and write about crabs or something easy, but I couldn't pull myself away. Water bears are like tiny, chubby aliens with eight legs, and they are literally everywhere on earth where there's water, even Antarctica. They're on the beach, in rain gutters, and everywhere else. You can see them if you look, but just barely, like flecks of salt. They freeze in ice, or get sent to space, or boiled, and after they recuperate, they're fine.

I asked the kids around me if they'd ever heard of them before, but no one had.

"Dude, I can't believe you found *another* bear," Ethan said. "That's so you. This should be your topic." Their scientific name was *tardigrade,* which means "slow walker" in Latin. I sighed. Just like me.

Sunlight dazzled me as I drove around the bend toward home after school. Everything lined up, and the sun shone down the road between the walls of trees like a river through a canyon. I barely caught a movement in the ditch off the road. I noticed a skirt that looked like it was made from a kid's sheet. And hair like a suncatcher. Izzy bent over when I passed, not even noticing the Rooster, a silver shooting star in all that light. I parked by the next driveway and hopped out.

She bent over, pulled at something, and put it in a basket. I jumped around to loosen up my leg. It scared a bunny across the road, but Izzy didn't look up until my shadow reached her. She started like a deer, even though I made noise.

"Hi." I raised my hand. "Doing some gardening?" I should have thought about something to say on the walk over. Something better, I mean. Izzy squinted into the glare.

"Hey, Newt! More like harvesting, I guess." She held out a basket full of green spirals.

"It looks like a snail and an asparagus had a baby."

"That would be awesome, and gross. They're fiddleheads,

baby fern fronds. You can eat them, at least the ostrich fern kind. But only if they're all wound up like this."

"How do they taste?"

"I haven't tried them yet. I'm going to cook half of them in butter and half of them in oil and garlic and see which is better." She held one up to me. "Want to try?"

"Yeah . . . no thanks. There is a spider on that one."

She bent down and held the papery coil against a cedar until the spider climbed onto the bark. Crab barrettes held her hair back from her face. Actual dead crabs, the size of chicken nuggets, with claws and everything.

"They have to be cooked anyway. Otherwise they're toxic." She dropped the coil back in the basket and looked up at me. "I wouldn't have let you eat it yet."

"How come you save a little spider but you wear dead things in your hair?"

"The crabs were already dead when I found them. I don't want to eat *or* wear the spider. You're wearing dead stuff on your feet, if you want to get technical."

I looked down, expecting squished ants or something.

"The leather," she said. "Most of us wear dead stuff all the time." She touched a crab barrette and smiled. I will never understand how weird people get on the island. "They're pretty. You just have to look at them in a different way."

"What else do you have in there?" I pointed at the basket. She pushed the fern babies aside.

"Some dandelion leaves—also reportedly edible—nettles, and thimbleberries. I tried the thimbleberries already, and they're delicious. Like raspberries." She offered me one.

"No thanks, I don't really like berries."

"It's like a gumdrop that sat in your pocket too long, but in a good way," she said as she ate it. Little raised scratches covered her hands.

"You should wear gloves in the brambles."

"I think I'm done for now." A car passed, and we moved farther into the ditch, just in case.

"Do you want a ride somewhere?" She tilted her head and stared at me.

"Sure, I'll take a ride. I'll get these in the fridge and look for more berries."

"A ride with a delinquent," I said as I unlocked the door. She took a step back. "I meant, you know, for driving the Rooster around with no license. That's all." I hopped in the driver's side and tried to make it look like it still didn't freak me out every time.

"The Rooster, huh? Is there a reward, by any chance? If a girl wants to do right by the world and turn in a scofflaw?" It took me a minute to answer, because I was thinking about the word *scofflaw*. I'd never heard it before, but it sounded dangerous. It was a good word.

"Good luck. I think as long as I make a solid effort not to run anyone over, I'm golden."

"Good to know." She reached out and touched a dial on the dashboard. "This is like a cockpit. A cockpit with fuzzy dice."

"A cockpit that smells like an armpit," I said. She snorted. "I thought *armpit* was a bad word until I was nine." She laughed with me or at me, but I guess it doesn't matter. "Where to? I mean, where are you staying?"

"You can drop me off in town. Maybe at Herb's? I could get a couple of things to go with the ferns. They might be better with some pecorino. That's a cheese." I pulled out into the wash of light on the road.

"Everything is better with cheese. But I can take you straight home if you want. It's no trouble. Was that your mom I saw you with the other day? The woman in the floppy hat?"

"Yeah, it was, actually. Can this thing fit over the bridge into Haven Cove?"

"I've never tried. Probably not. You must be staying with the Watsons." They owned the best, and only, bakery on Murphy. They didn't have kids, so she must be a niece or something. Haven Cove was a little circle of old cottages that Truman

Murphy built around a pretty little lagoon for the resort's star performers long ago. Now the cottages were mostly run-down vacation rentals. "I can take you to the bridge, at least. Do you go to Lincoln Bay?"

"I'm not sure where I'm going next year," Izzy said.

She told me about making pesto out of nettles she found near Jamila Park. I knew the patch she talked about. It was the size of a baseball diamond, at the turn in the path. Chuck and I avoided it, because nettles sting if you touch the bottoms of the leaves barehanded, but Izzy went there on purpose. She said her grandma taught her mom how to collect the nettles, and her mom taught her. She wore gloves and said cooking washes the sting out.

Then she said, "Newt, are you all right? You've got rings around your eyes."

"I'm just tired." She looked worried, so I said, "Tired of driving."

"Why didn't you pick something easier to drive?"

"My parents got it for me," I said.

"Lucky you." I rolled my eyes and dropped Izzy off by the Haven Cove bridge on my way into town.

CHAPTER 13

Herb's Market used to be a resort gymnasium, but now it's the grocery store. One of Lyric's posters was already in the window between a constellation map and my Huxley flyer. An old lady was weighing more zucchini than I want to eat in my lifetime. I avoided the berries, like I had all year, but my neck hairs stood up when I caught sight of something yellow off to the side, near the parsley and sprouts. Not really yellow but mustard-colored. I recognized the jacket first. Velvet. Fancy. The guy Little Leti talked to on the ferry was standing near the yams. He still had that old drive-in-movies hair. His arms were crossed, and he wore mirrored sunglasses inside. I looked down at a tray of apples, but I could still see him. He wasn't moving, or shopping, or turning away. He took off his sunglasses and stared right at me. I looked at him straight on, and he nodded. I tried to shop like normal. I followed the lines of shuffleboard courts along the floor. Mr. Mustard stayed back but also kept an eye on me. I went through Mom's list: jam, bread, nut butter, kale, Havarti cheese, raisins. He pointed at me, and I dropped the box of raisins. They scattered across the floor.

"Hey, buddy." Herb the grocer squatted down. "Let me get that." He walked down the aisle to get a broom. One time Ethan threw a bag of chips through the basketball hoop and it got stuck in the net. Herb made us climb a ladder to see the top of the freezers with all the stuff people tossed through the basket. Bags of nuts. Keys. Tubes of toothpaste.

"Are you all right, Newt?" He hugged the handle of the broom against his apron. Octopus tattoos trail down each arm and he has a bullring in his nose. He lets us keep a tab that my parents settle after payday.

"I'm fine," I said. I scooped the raisins around me in a pile. We stood alone in the aisle. I leaned toward him and whispered, "Did you see a guy wearing a yellow jacket?"

"Was he bothering you?" Herb tightened his grip on the broom handle and looked at me harder. When he was a teenager, Herb went to juvie for fighting in Lincoln.

"Not exactly," I said. "He was watching me. He stood by the vegetables, and he pointed at me." Herb rubbed his cheek. His gray whiskers sounded like Velcro.

"Maybe he was curious about what you were buying. A lot of people watching goes on in here. Some Murphers don't have the best social skills."

"I don't think he's a Murpher. I've only seen him twice. Once on the ferry to Lincoln and now here." Herb nodded and swept up stray raisins.

"Well, we get lots of visitors. You should know by now that almost anything can start to seem normal around here. Like, say, a twelve-year-old with a big truck. You have it here with you today, by any chance?"

"I'm thirteen. Why?"

"I need to get snacks and drinks up to Neighbor Hall for the festival volunteers as soon as possible, but I have a lot to do around here." He smiled and looked at the mess of raisins I made. "It's on your way home."

"Isn't everything on the way home if the main road is one loop?" I said.

"I'll throw in some cookies." Herb grabbed a pack of oat-meal chocolate chip pecans from the top shelf.

"Deal."

Mr. Mustard glared at me on my way to the register, and

I stared back. Herb waved at him, and Mr. Mustard nodded and read the side of a box of couscous. I should have told Herb that it felt wrong, but maybe he was right and Mr. Mustard was a Murpher who didn't like kids. Or maybe Herb would lose his temper and do something to get in trouble. I bagged my groceries while Herb stacked bagels, cream cheese, fruit, and chips in a couple of old crates. I petted Achilles and Patroclus, Herb's two rescued corgis, who have wheels for back legs. They nap in the back once they get tired of people's attention. I had a wheelchair for a few weeks after the attack, and Herb said we were a matched set.

"Can you help me out to the truck with this stuff?" I said. I could have managed, but a muscled escort was a good thing. Mr. Mustard didn't follow us out. Herb walked his dolly of crates to the Rooster, and I unlocked the back doors.

"Drive carefully," he said. "Save the cookies for when you're parked." I promised I would. Mr. Mustard left the store and walked around the corner in the other direction, but Herb had his head in the truck and didn't see. I left before Mr. Mustard came back.

I wasn't ready to go back inside the theater. Last year, Ethan and I rehearsed there over and over. Dad rigged wires for sound, Leti passed him cables, and Mom and her friends practiced an act with twenty LED Hula-Hoops. They laughed a lot, because they still needed practice, but it was okay. Three days later, I didn't watch where I was going in the brambles and everything changed.

Now a guy walked on stilts over the grass next to the lake while a couple of women practiced a fake-fighting acrobatics routine under an old oak tree like it was a big fringy circus tent. Other people took turns showing off magic tricks. The old me would have been right in the circle with them.

Going through the backstage door made my heart jump. I worried that the crates would slip out of my sweaty grip as I passed hoop jugglers, dancers, and a guy rigging a high wire across the stage. I know my way around the theater. I know how to get through the backstage passages, how to find the secret bathroom that never has a line, and where to watch my step so I won't trip. I took a deep breath and tried to soak up what makes the place special, but it just smelled dusty. I set the crates on a table by the stage and watched Tom-with-the-beard from the paddleboats bend spoons until Gilda spotted me.

"Newt! Oh, man, it's so good to see you. How are you feeling?" She stepped forward like she was going to hug me, but she stopped and put her hands in her pockets. "Did you come with your mom?" She looked around.

"Just me." An assistant in a kilt brought her a clipboard. Gilda whispered in the assistant's ear, and he nodded and left.

"I'm so glad you're back. I'll always find space for you. You practically grew up here. What would you like to do?"

"I'm not here to perform. I'm just dropping off food from Herb." Friends of my mom's practiced juggling while someone cartwheeled through the break in the spinning clubs. They laughed every time the cartwheeler got clubbed. One waved but I turned away.

"If you want to sign up, the last few slots are going fast." Gilda had that wild look she got whenever it was almost showtime. I shook my head and set out the drinks. "We need lots of help backstage and in the front of the house too. Talk to Adam. Maybe you could be an usher."

"Maybe." I didn't want to be an usher either. What would my parents say about me being there? Dad tried to get Mom to sign up again, but he wasn't exactly down here helping to build sets.

Musky climbed out of the orchestra pit. "Newt! Guess what? I found it. The wish worked!" Musky walked toward us, and I got goosebumps.

"I wished on Newt's bear to find my wedding ring." Gilda tilted her head in confusion, and Musky kept talking. "It'd been gone for a month! But after I wished, I looked up and there it was, in the tree!" The bigger Musky's smile, the more uncomfortable I got.

"I went outside with my orange pekoe tea, the way I do

every night after work. I noticed something catching the light up in the branches. I figured it could be trash or something that the wind blew in, right? Maybe tinsel from someone's old Christmas tree. I took a closer look." Musky paused with his arms out for dramatic effect. "The chain was tangled around a branch, and the ring twirled in the breeze. I went inside to grab a ladder and pulled it down. Chain's busted, but the ring is good as new." He held out his hand as proof.

"It was gone for a month, and then you saw it hanging right in your yard?" Gilda said.

"Yeah." Musky barked a laugh. "Maybe a bird saw it and put it in its nest? Sometimes they like shiny things, right?" Musky punched me on the shoulder. "I only know that this guy rolled up with that bear and his wishbone and"—he made a *poof* motion with his hands—"my wish came true!"

Gilda looked at me like I had the next line. "Is this a joke?"

"You would have found it anyway, right?" I said. "That's where you drink your tea."

"Who knows? I sit there every day, and I never saw it. Anyway, thank that bear of yours for me, all right?" Musky saluted us and headed backstage.

"Bear? What's he talking about, Newt?" Gilda looked down at my legs and covered her mouth.

"Just a wooden statue that washed up. It doesn't have

anything to do with . . . that. Musky thinks it's lucky, I guess,"
I said. "It's no big deal. I've got to go."

Gilda came over to the house a few times after the attack to
bring food and see if we needed anything. But Mom stopped
answering the door. She wouldn't even talk to her. For a while,
Gilda left casseroles and soups on the ski swing on the porch.

I climbed into the truck and closed my eyes. Ethan, Carlos,
Lyric, and Musky all got their wishes. I looked at Huxley, and
my neck felt tickly.

If he actually *was* magic, I could wish too. I didn't want to
believe it, but maybe if I just told Huxley what I really wanted,
he could make it happen. I could move to Lincoln. Everything
would be better. I got a warm, floaty feeling. I sat up straighter
and laughed out loud. Sitting in the Rooster next to a maybe-
magic bear, surrounded by people practicing circus acts, I felt
closer to normal than I had in a long time.

CHAPTER 14

The next morning, I woke up from another dream and tried to anchor myself to real life. I hummed. I ran my hands over the stitching in my quilt. I looked at the photos on my corkboard and old festival posters on the walls, but it all felt like someone else's room.

Parrots in the cherry tree outside my window squawked when I pulled my curtain back. Maybe they weren't upset. Maybe conversations are hard to have with a beak. I slowly opened the window. It didn't make any noise that I could hear, but the parrots quieted all at once. They shifted on branches, little green and red and yellow heads tilted toward me, dark eyes blinking.

"Hello . . ." A few hopped from foot to foot. "Hello . . .

hello . . . hello," I said over and over, low and slow. I paused for a few seconds each time in case any of them wanted to say it back. I held my breath and waited for one to try. Maybe I could leave little treats on the windowsill like Mom does for the crows. They could have grapes or apple slices when the cherries are gone.

I could get to know them, maybe name them. People in town would get used to hearing parrots talking to each other up in the trees. I leaned out the window. "Hello," I said again. They looked away, and on an invisible cue, the flock took off together and shook the leaves. The wind from their wings brushed my face as they launched up into a sky as blue as anything could ever hope to be. They turned into specks like sky dust, microscopic birds headed toward the springs, farther and farther away.

Downstairs, Dad stared out the kitchen window. He didn't know I was there until I opened the cupboard for a cereal bowl. He'd been working on a building that was behind schedule and I had barely seen him for three days. He made oatmeal and asked how it went with Musky. I didn't tell him about Mr. Mustard at Herb's. He didn't need anything else to worry about. I told him about Huxley, but he'd already seen Musky's ring. He just laughed about the wishes.

"What do you think about Manxadon getting a bubble helmet to go underwater?"

"For what?"

"To help Marvelo fight the Moneywort warriors in the Undercity," he said without even cracking a smile.

I jumped when he slammed the cupboard I'd left open.

"Relax, mijo." He squeezed my shoulder.

"There's a city in the lake now?" He took a conversation about a bear with wish juju and made it even weirder.

"I want to introduce it now, and it can be more of a feature in the second volume."

"Right. Do you want to make a wish?" I asked. "Maybe for your project to get done?"

"Ha, maybe later. What about you, Newt? Did you make a wish?"

"I didn't. Not yet," I said. He filled his favorite to-go cup with black coffee. "It's strange, though, right? That people would think it could be magic or something?" I wanted someone to say it was absurd, because it felt possible, and that wasn't right. "What would you wish for, Dad?" Maybe he would say to quit his job.

"What do I need wishes for?" he said. "I've got everything I want right here."

I smiled back at him. "You don't believe wishing works?"

He looked thoughtful as he drank his coffee.

"Wishing doesn't hurt. But I like to focus on what's here

and now." He followed my eyes to the Marvelo comic on the fridge. "Usually."

"What about birthday candles? What do you think about, if you're not wishing?"

"Cake." He handed me my lunch. "I'll drop you off at school on my way to work."

I went to the library and worked on the brochure homework. I watched videos and read a dozen articles about water bears. They've been found in the Himalayas and the desert. Some had been dried up for eight years, and they still come back to life. Scientists just found a new species in a puddle in Japan. Murphy Island is so soggy, it's probably a water bear metropolis. I wrote a rough paragraph before the bell rang.

Rocket's friend Dylan sat with Ethan and me at lunch. He said his sister says they have tacos and pizza in the cafeteria at Lincoln Bay. On Murphy, everybody packs a lunch.

"That sounds amazing," I said.

"Everyone knows school cafeteria food isn't that good," Ethan said. "We're lucky we don't have to eat it." He packed up his sandwich and left. I watched him walk around the rim of the pool, scowling at us the whole way.

I didn't get to talk to him again until after school.

"Listen." I sighed. "Somebody made another wish on the bear. And it came true."

He nodded. "Let's wait until we can talk somewhere more private," he said, even though nobody was around. "Low tide is minus three in an hour. You up for a walk to the beach?"

I hadn't walked that far since my leg got chewed, but I could handle it. Ethan went ahead of me, not even slowing down the whole way. But he looked calmer once we got there.

The water pulled the sand, and the sand pulled our feet. I rolled up my pants and waded in to cool the ache in my knee. Ethan watched, but concerned, not staring.

"I don't see your imaginary girlfriend," he said. My cheeks got hot, but I didn't take his bait.

"Musky wished on the bear to find his wedding ring. He found it right afterward."

"What?" Ethan moved sugar kelp off an old brick and turned it over with a stick. "So that's three. Me, Lyric, and now Musky."

"Four. Carlos wished for a raise, and then he got one." I snagged a sandwich bag that was drifting toward an orange jellyfish. I put it in my pocket to throw out later.

"Admit it," said Ethan. "There's something awesome happening!"

"Something funny *is* going on." My feet slurped. I tried not to let on how hard it was to balance in the incoming tide.

"No kidding! You have to make a wish. What do you want? A new knee?" Ethan scooped up a handful of sand.

"A new life," I said. No magic could change the past, but if I was somewhere new, like at my grandma's, everything could be different.

"What?" Ethan dropped the maybe-golden sand, and I held my breath. If I didn't tell him now and he found out from someone else, he'd hate me forever.

"Don't get mad. I've been thinking I could wish to leave. Not just to go to Lincoln Bay but to move off of Murphy. At least for the summer. But if I liked it, I could maybe stay in Lincoln, since my grandma's house isn't too far. I would still come back and visit. And you could come see me in Lincoln."

His face twisted up, and I had to turn away. I picked sand off my hands like I was thinking about it. "I'm sorry, but nothing has felt right since last summer. Something needs to change. But I'll miss you a lot." My throat burned. Ethan's best friend before me moved away.

Ethan smiled at me, but it didn't spread around his face. The parrots screeched somewhere over the bluff.

"Just figure out if that's what you really want, because you only get one chance," he said.

"What do you mean?"

"I didn't want to tell you until you believed." Ethan threw another handful of sand into the surf and cleared his throat.

"The bear only gives one wish per person. I tried another one. I enunciated, just in case I mumbled for the hedgehog wish." He turned over a piece of driftwood. I squinted out at the waves. Little pieces of broken day floated away.

"What did you wish for?" I thought I already knew, but I asked anyway.

"I thought I could wish to have my dad back. Or to miss him less. I don't know how strong the bear magic is. And I worried that it would be another half wish and I'd make it worse somehow. But I wished anyway." Tiny waves reflected in his shiny eyes. I could barely hear, but I think he said, "I had to."

"What happened?"

"It didn't work. Nothing changed." He bit his lip. "I wasted my chance before we knew for sure. What if my dad knew I could change things, to get him back, and I wished for a hedgehog?" He squatted down and dug the heels of his hands into his eyes.

"I think he'd like Boxwood," I said, but he shook his head. It hurt to look at him. Sometimes sadness comes out of someone like breath, even when they don't talk. Especially when they don't talk at all.

"I'm sorry, Ethan. It must be awful to miss him so much." He already had more missing than most kids should have to deal with, and now I was going to make it worse.

"Some days it's fine. Other days I feel guilty that it's fine. And other days . . ." He tucked his chin down and sniffed. I waited for him to say more, but he stood up and wiped his hands over his face. "That leaves two possibilities." He held out two fingers. "The bear is selective in which wishes he grants—"

"Like there's no way he could bring your dad back. He probably can't change something that already happened."

"Exactly, and he couldn't stop what happened to you last year. The other possibility is that I only got one wish, and I used it on Boxwood. So maybe think about it real hard before you wish to get away from here."

"All right." I nodded. I could wish for a bike instead of the truck, or for my leg not to hurt, or to never have another dream about it again, but none of that felt like enough. The tiniest hope that I could change everything made me feel like all the little pieces of warm light came off the water and washed over me. "So people should be careful what they wish for. Maybe we shouldn't let people tell the bear their wishes."

"Settle down, commander," Ethan said. "You can't stop people from making wishes. This isn't a dystopian wasteland. Are we all going to start wearing gray jumpsuits and get divided into factions?" He combed through the sand.

"What have you been reading?" I laughed, but he kept

frowning. "We shouldn't tell them about the bear. About your theory about the bear."

"The bear is out of the bag, man," he said. "People are going to find out. Unless we put him back in the water, they're going to keep wishing around him." I wanted to keep Huxley just for me. Not because of any magic, but I liked talking to him. Ethan held up a sandy C shape, about the size of a plate.

"Do you know that moon snails protect their eggs by making casings like this out of sand and mucus? Sometimes people think they're plastic litter and throw them away. They disintegrate, and thousands of moon snail babies are born." Ethan laid the casing gently back onto the sand and headed down the beach. I didn't follow. We left after he found a rusty lunch box and a rubber duck with Japanese writing on it. He wanted to look up the writing online. I wanted to go home.

The next morning I put dishes away while Mom made soap. I used to help her. I liked smelling the vanilla and lemon mint she adds. And I liked to pop the soap out of the molds. I don't volunteer now, and she doesn't ask. She's around more, but we're together less. She still wore her vest from work.

"Mom, what would you wish for?" I asked. She mixed

milk and lye and oils together until it all looked like cake batter. Enough time passed that I thought she wouldn't answer.

She stirred the mixture. "What do you mean?"

"If you had a wish, what would you use it on?" I watered the sad little avocado pit on the windowsill. Mom plants them, but it's always the same: the pit grows a stick with a couple of long leaves before it notices that it's not warm here and dies. Maybe she would wish for an avocado tree. Or for all of us to go to Mexico. Or New York, where she could ride the subway like she did in college. She told me about the turnstiles, the crowds moving together lower and lower under the city, the *whoosh* of air as trains rattled by. She could be reminded of how everyone leaned together as the train rocked through dark tunnels, barreling toward a hundred different adventures. She loved it.

Mom peeled her glove back and scratched the faded D.S. tattoo on the base of her thumb. I asked her what it was when I was younger, and she said it stood for "cautionary tale." She likes mysteries.

"Don't we always have wishes?" She held out her hand for a clean spoon.

"Well, sure. But what would you wish for if it was a *real* wish? If you knew it would come true?" I said, and passed her the spoon.

"Maybe you shouldn't wish for anything unless you want it to come true," she said.

She poured the soap into little round molds. A new goat milagro hung with the others on the purple ribbon, probably for Margie's cold. Mom had a new flaming heart too.

Leti came in with a pencil and a notebook "Did the mail come yet?"

"Not yet."

"How do you spell *indubitably*?" she asked.

"What are you working on, Let?" I told her how to spell it. I think.

"I've got a new pen pal in Texas!" She hugged the notebook to her chest. "Some of them don't write back that often, so it's okay." She went back to the dining room table. Sometimes she adds drawings or stickers to the letters.

"Why would you have only one wish?" Mom asked.

"That's the rule. You have to use it on something important. Something that would make your life better." I took a deep breath and said it. "Ethan thinks the wooden bear I found on the beach grants wishes."

I stayed quiet while she stamped shapes into the line of soaps down the counter. Feathers and milagros and little coils of wire imprinted on each circle of soap. She'd give them to neighbors, and we'd get salmon, fruit, maybe an oil change or some hand-me-down clothes.

"One wish. Well, in that case, I would wish to fly." She took off the gloves and held her arms out like wings and flew out of the kitchen.

I finished the dishes. Mom's sewing machine rattled and hummed in the basement. I guess she expected me to put everything away and wipe up the soap spills. I started to, but I left the mess behind.

My grandma sent a card with a cartoon of a horse eating grass that said, "Just a little hay." She wrote about having lunch with my tías and planting beans and corn in the garden. She also slipped in a coupon for an ice cream place in Lincoln, thinking we might like a treat next time we visited. I traced my finger over her careful cursive before sticking the card up on the refrigerator.

CHAPTER 15

On Wednesday night, there was a knock at the door. Mom was on her sewing machine in the basement again, and Dad was sketching at the kitchen table in his favorite flannel pants. He says they help him feel creative.

"I'll get it," I said, but I don't know if he heard me.

I peeked through the curtains at a truck I didn't recognize parked behind the Rooster. "Hi," I said, and cracked the door open.

"Hey, there . . . sport." A tall guy with a big beard stood on the porch. He wore a big leather hat, with a feather and some sort of animal tail tied to the band. I'd seen him before. He works the counter at the pizza parlor.

"Can I help you?" I said. Chuck sat behind the guy, wag-ging his tail. He's a terrible watchdog.

"I'm here about the flyer. I'm Henry. I tried to call, but nobody answered. Someone found a bear?"

"I did." I cleared my throat. "It washed up on the beach. Not a real bear. Like one of those chainsaw carvings?" He pumped his fist into the air, and my heart sank. "Did you, uh, lose one? A bear?"

"Yep, couple months back. One night I got home from work and he was on my porch steps as usual, and the next morning he was gone. You say you found him?"

"My friend and I found him on Echo Beach."

"Not sure how he got down there." He laughed. I laughed along with him, but I had questions.

"Is the bear, I've been calling him Huxley, is he—"

"Walter."

"What?"

"His name is Walter," Henry said.

"All right, is Walter . . . special?" I looked at Henry and tried to show with my eyes that I meant *special.*

"Of course. I made him myself from a big leaf maple that came down in a storm three or four winters ago," Henry said. "Where is he?"

"He's out in my truck—our family's truck. Right over

here." I pointed toward it while I slipped on my flip-flops. We crossed the yard, Chuck trailing behind us. I should have lied and said there was no bear. Or maybe it was better this way. Huxley would leave with this giant man with a tail, and the nonsense with the wishes would be over. But I wouldn't have him to talk to anymore, and I never got to make my wish.

"Took me three weeks after work to carve him. I don't know why I did it. I never did nothing like that before. But I figured, how hard can it be?" The man shrugged. I tried again.

"How did he get to be . . . you know. Like he is?"

"Not sure I catch your drift," Henry said. He didn't want to talk about it. I nodded to show that I understood and I was cool with it. We walked down the driveway in silence.

"Maybe I can visit? Walter, I mean. Come and see him sometimes?" I asked. The man adjusted the brim of his hat and looked at me sideways.

"Probably best if Walter and I get on our way," he said.

"All right, but what harm would it do if he's sitting on your porch steps? I wouldn't bother you or anything."

"I'd like to get my bear back now, please," he said. It was silly. There was nothing special about the bear. There couldn't be, and now it would be over as soon as he took it. I opened the back door of the Rooster. Huxley—I couldn't call him

Walter—stood right there like he couldn't wait to hop out and walk away with this man.

"What's this?"

"It used to be a taco truck."

"No, where's Walter?"

"Right there." I pointed, but the man shook his head.

"That there's a fine bear, but he's not *my* bear. Walter's smaller and his face is different. More smiley. His arms and legs are different too."

"Wait—this isn't your bear?"

"Nope." The man sighed. "I should have mounted him down with rebar."

"This isn't Walter!" I yelled, like I won an argument. "Whose bear is it?"

"I guess it's yours," he said. He talked about the craftsmanship and chainsaw technique, and I couldn't stop smiling. He apologized for the mix-up and said he'd tell anybody missing a bear where to find us. He tipped his tail hat and left. Mom limped across the grass toward me.

"Are you okay?" I called. She said yeah, but she winced when her foot caught on a rut.

"Who was that?"

I explained, and she headed back to the house. Huxley could stay. I gave him a little hug, careful not to catch my hands on any barnacles.

"You're a water bear," I told him. I couldn't stop smiling. If they sent Huxley to space, he'd probably come back just the same, like the tardigrades.

I fed and cuddled the goats and hung around in the truck with Huxley until Carlos called. "Can we visit abuela?" I said. "Maybe we could shoot hoops at that park by Lincoln Bay?"

"Oh, man, I'd love that, but my buddy Jonah is in town, so a few of the guys are getting together. How about next week? Ask Mom and Dad if you can spend the night at my place. You could stay for the weekend." I said I would, and we made plans for pizza and go-karts. Maybe by then I could tell him that I was coming for good. I couldn't wait.

Ethan came over after dinner. He'd been avoiding me ever since I told him about moving. Every time he looked at me at school, I felt like a traitor. But tonight, he just looked resigned.

"My mom went to pub trivia. Let's go to the lake," he said. Ethan's backpack was full with a camera and stakeout supplies.

"It's late."

"So? We only have a few more days of school until summer vacation. Come on!"

I didn't want to go, but I grabbed my water bottle and hoodie. We parked the Rooster between some willows. I locked

...ise grew, like a chorus of mumbly whining. My stomach

...d up. Maybe Dad really did see something.

...ewt? There's more than one." Ethan sat up.

...n-human voices came from the lake. Two and three dif-

...calls, like a chorus. Dad's outrageous stories might be

...could be wrong about everything. My leg cramped. I felt

...slowly slipping down the bank toward the murky water.

...spot in the middle of the lake grew darker as something

...d toward the light. There was a whine, like a nervous

..., and the water sloshed. Darkness makes everything

...r. The water below the bank was probably deep enough

...mething big to get close.

...et's go." I pulled on Ethan's sleeve, but he shook me off.

...ed to focus the camera.

...his could be our only chance," he said.

...here's nothing there. There can't be." My mouth felt

...nd I wanted to run, even with the cramp in my leg. More

...sloshed. A familiar, doleful sound rolled over the water

...shore. Ethan shushed me and leaned forward.

...see the neck! It looks like . . ." Something came into

...but not a scaly monster. A paddleboat, the bigger swan,

...d over the water. It could have come loose from the dock,

...hadowy shapes moved inside. Rowdy teenagers.

...mething bleated. Like a goat. My goat.

...he supernova path lights caught the inside of the swan

the doors, and we walked around to the boggy side of the lake again. We picked a new spot behind cattails with a better view of the water. We waited. I didn't see anybody else around. My butt went to sleep, and fog rose on the water, but it was only us, bats, and mosquitos again. Dogs barked on the other side of the lake, a plane flew by, and we waited.

"Rocket says we should go camping, but I told him you probably wouldn't want to do it," Ethan said.

"Nope."

"Did you make your wish yet? I only ask because you're still here."

"Not yet. Soon."

"You could wish for school to be over already."

"We only have one more week," I said.

"Maybe you should wish for world peace," Ethan said.

"No," I said. "That's what *everybody* wishes for."

"But not everybody has a magical bear that grants wishes. We could change the world," he said.

"It won't work. It'll waste a wish." I realized how loud I was and whispered, "Most people on the island would wish for peace if you told them to make an important wish. Look at everyone's bumper stickers."

He pulled the hood of his sweatshirt up and his sleeves down over his hands. "My mom says another storm is coming."

"The beach will have new junk." That perked him up a

little. I pictured a line of wooden bears down the sand, scattered like driftwood.

Ethan said, "The whole island could wish for peace together."

I sighed. "Wishes don't work that way. Peace probably doesn't either."

"Why not?"

"It's too much? It sounds like 'whirled peas.' We could wind up getting that for lunch for the last week of school! Besides, if that could work, wouldn't it have worked by now? People wish for peace on birthday candles, shooting stars, and everything else. With Huxley, it probably has to be something smaller, more personal." I waved a moth away.

"It seems like a wasted chance. How else can we get world peace?"

"Don't be a jerk? Spread kindness. Be patient and respectful. All that stuff. You have to work for it, not wish for it. Promise me you won't get someone to spend their wish on that, all right? I'll help you do something else for peace."

"Like what?"

"We can deliver flowers in the Rooster. Or soup or something. People love soup. It's soothing."

"You're not going to stick around for that once you use your wish." I couldn't see Ethan, but I heard the sadness in his voice. "What are you waiting for?"

I wanted to explain, but I didn't kno
thing moved on the lake.

I sat up and held a finger to my lips
era out of his backpack so slowly, it di
reached up and pulled a leafy branch
whatever was in the water.

"Should we go?" Ethan mouthed.
whispers, like my brain talking to itself
say yes, but I remembered there was n
There is no Marvelo.

"There cannot be a magic bear *an*
doesn't work like that, even here. You'll

Ethan shook his head and said, "Y
should have rules and make sense."

"So?"

"It doesn't." He glared at me so har
"The world is full of things we can't exp
tell him something I read about the tardig
live near ocean volcanos, but he ruine
yetis, crop circles. You can't explain how

I tucked one reed around another for
lake. More splashing, and a murmuring
toward us. I squinted into the dark but
Everything but the noise from the lake fe
ther back, and Ethan did too. Water sla

the no
knott

"N
N
ferent
real. I
mysel

A
pushe
anima
loude
for s

"I
He tr
"
"
dry a
water
to the

"
view,
glide
but s

S
T

the doors, and we walked around to the boggy side of the lake again. We picked a new spot behind cattails with a better view of the water. We waited. I didn't see anybody else around. My butt went to sleep, and fog rose on the water, but it was only us, bats, and mosquitos again. Dogs barked on the other side of the lake, a plane flew by, and we waited.

"Rocket says we should go camping, but I told him you probably wouldn't want to do it," Ethan said.

"Nope."

"Did you make your wish yet? I only ask because you're still here."

"Not yet. Soon."

"You could wish for school to be over already."

"We only have one more week," I said.

"Maybe you should wish for world peace," Ethan said.

"No," I said. "That's what *everybody* wishes for."

"But not everybody has a magical bear that grants wishes. We could change the world," he said.

"It won't work. It'll waste a wish." I realized how loud I was and whispered, "Most people on the island would wish for peace if you told them to make an important wish. Look at everyone's bumper stickers."

He pulled the hood of his sweatshirt up and his sleeves down over his hands. "My mom says another storm is coming."

"The beach will have new junk." That perked him up a

little. I pictured a line of wooden bears down the sand, scattered like driftwood.

Ethan said, "The whole island could wish for peace together."

I sighed. "Wishes don't work that way. Peace probably doesn't either."

"Why not?"

"It's too much? It sounds like 'whirled peas.' We could wind up getting that for lunch for the last week of school! Besides, if that could work, wouldn't it have worked by now? People wish for peace on birthday candles, shooting stars, and everything else. With Huxley, it probably has to be something smaller, more personal." I waved a moth away.

"It seems like a wasted chance. How else can we get world peace?"

"Don't be a jerk? Spread kindness. Be patient and respectful. All that stuff. You have to work for it, not wish for it. Promise me you won't get someone to spend their wish on that, all right? I'll help you do something else for peace."

"Like what?"

"We can deliver flowers in the Rooster. Or soup or something. People love soup. It's soothing."

"You're not going to stick around for that once you use your wish." I couldn't see Ethan, but I heard the sadness in his voice. "What are you waiting for?"

I wanted to explain, but I didn't know how. But then something moved on the lake.

I sat up and held a finger to my lips. Ethan pulled the camera out of his backpack so slowly, it didn't make any noise. I reached up and pulled a leafy branch down, hiding us from whatever was in the water.

"Should we go?" Ethan mouthed. It was the slightest of whispers, like my brain talking to itself. Part of me wanted to say yes, but I remembered there was nothing to be scared of. There is no Marvelo.

"There cannot be a magic bear *and* a lake serpent. Life doesn't work like that, even here. You'll see," I said.

Ethan shook his head and said, "You act like everything should have rules and make sense."

"So?"

"It doesn't." He glared at me so hard, I had to look away. "The world is full of things we can't explain." I was about to tell him something I read about the tardigrades, how they even live near ocean volcanos, but he ruined it. "Ghosts, UFOs, yetis, crop circles. You can't explain how, but they're there."

I tucked one reed around another for a clearer view of the lake. More splashing, and a murmuring-crying sound came toward us. I squinted into the dark but only saw dark blobs. Everything but the noise from the lake felt still. I scooted farther back, and Ethan did too. Water slapped the shore, and the noise grew, like a chorus of mumbly whining. My stomach knotted up. Maybe Dad really did see something.

"Newt? There's more than one." Ethan sat up.

Non-human voices came from the lake. Two and three different calls, like a chorus. Dad's outrageous stories might be real. I could be wrong about everything. My leg cramped. I felt myself slowly slipping down the bank toward the murky water.

A spot in the middle of the lake grew darker as something pushed toward the light. There was a whine, like a nervous animal, and the water sloshed. Darkness makes everything louder. The water below the bank was probably deep enough for something big to get close.

"Let's go." I pulled on Ethan's sleeve, but he shook me off. He tried to focus the camera.

"This could be our only chance," he said.

"There's nothing there. There can't be." My mouth felt dry and I wanted to run, even with the cramp in my leg. More water sloshed. A familiar, doleful sound rolled over the water to the shore. Ethan *shush*ed me and leaned forward.

"I see the neck! It looks like . . ." Something came into view, but not a scaly monster. A paddleboat, the bigger swan, glided over the water. It could have come loose from the dock, but shadowy shapes moved inside. Rowdy teenagers.

Something bleated. Like a goat. My goat.

The supernova path lights caught the inside of the swan

boat and showed my mother in multicolor. At least three goats stood in the boat, and Chuck sat shotgun. I felt like I was trying to breathe through a wet washcloth. The funny thing is, it all looked normal. The goats even seemed calm, and I wouldn't have guessed that they would ever be all right with a boat ride. They glided past in almost total silence as a million questions swirled in my brain. How did they get to the lake? Had my mom done this before? It seemed like it. Speckles stretched her neck down to sniff the water. She got a little drink and jerked her head back into the boat.

Maybe other people knew Mom did this and didn't say anything, but probably not. She keeps her own secrets. Ethan looked back and forth between me and the boat. We watched her from the shadows, without talking, as if spying into a secret room. He lifted his camera again and looked through the lens but didn't take a picture. He put it back in his lap and sighed through gritted teeth. Mom wasn't searching for Marvelo. She looked straight ahead or up at the stars. She seemed happy, humming to the goats, petting Chuck's ears, and drifting around in the middle of Gertrude Lake. She was going for a ride, with three goats and a dog at night. We sat still, hidden by the cattails, and watched until she drifted away. Once the boat was out of sight around the bend, I breathed. Mud oozed through the knees of my pants and around my fingers, but I didn't stop moving away from the water until I stood on the path.

"Newt, what is going on? What was she doing out there?"

I looked at my best friend under the rainbow lights of the supernova safety portal, and I told him the truth.

"I don't know."

I woke up on the couch early Friday morning in a haze of bear, teeth, brambles, and something else, like a sticky coat of paint on a dumpster full of scrap and nails. I listened for anyone coming, in case I had yelled, but the house was quiet, even the squirrels. Dad is a heavy sleeper, and usually the first one in bed, but sometimes I wake up Mom or Leti. I smelled coffee.

Dad sat at the table, typing, wearing his flannel pants of creativity again. I looked over his shoulder. Marvelo stories.

"Good morning, mijo." He looked up and yawned.

"Dad, something happened," I said. "I think I saw Mom on the lake last night." I got a lopsided nectarine out of the bowl on the table and bit it. It tasted bland and stringy, so I tossed it in the compost bin.

"Huh." He typed. "It must have been somebody who looked like her."

"Well, um." I swallowed. "I don't think so. She was in a paddleboat. With Chuck, and some of the goats." He typed more.

"Where was this?"

"At the lake, last night with Ethan," I said. His fingers stopped, and he looked at me.

"What were you guys doing at the lake?"

I didn't want to say it, but I couldn't think of anything better to say. "Ethan wanted to look for Marvelo."

"You guys shouldn't be out there so late," he said. "It's not safe. I thought we could go together soon."

"You were working," I said.

He went back to typing. "Did you see anything?"

"Only Mom."

"It sounds like maybe your eyes played tricks on you in the dark." He closed the computer.

"I don't think so. It was her," I said. The clock ticked like a countdown in the hallway.

He refilled his coffee. "But why, though? Hmm? She wouldn't have any reason to be out there. The boat's not even working right now. I'm waiting for a timing belt."

"It was a paddleboat. The swan."

"I'm thinking of heading down to the lake for a while to catch video of Marvelo before work tomorrow," he said. "Want to come with? Maybe go for a swim?" I hadn't swum since before the attack. There are too many people, and cold water stings my scars and makes them redder. Ethan and I used to swim at the spring pools all the time—they're open year-round with the hot springs—but now I can't relax, thinking about people staring at my leg. It's something he should probably know about me.

"I can't. I've got a friend coming over."

"Ethan? Bring him too. Come on." I didn't correct him, and he got up and stashed his papers in his special spot in the cupboard. "We'll find some clues to what you saw last night. You can show me your stakeout spot."

"Stop ignoring me! I know what I saw," I said.

"All right." He sighed. "I can't talk about this right now, Newton." He pulled his sweatshirt over his head and picked up his stuff.

"Dad."

"Clean up your boxes in the hall before school, all right? They're upsetting your mother."

"Dad!" His footsteps faded down the hallway, and the house sat still.

At school, Ethan was quiet until the middle of lunch. He didn't wait for me outside before class, and he didn't want to see what I wrote about water bears. I turned in my paragraph for the brochure to Mrs. Ribchester and went to lunch. Ethan was already at our lunch table. He chewed each bite of his lentil burger for a long time. Finally, he sighed.

"I'm confused. Are your parents trying to make a hoax?

Your mom floats around out there, and your dad says he saw Marvelo?"

"I think they're separate," I said. "She wasn't trying to look like Marvelo. I don't want to talk about it."

"Is it for the reward?"

"They don't care about that stuff," I said. I stirred my fork in the fried rice Mom had packed, but I wasn't hungry.

"Then what? To get more tourists here? It won't work."

"They don't care about money *or* tourists, you know that," I said. They cared about money, but not the way he meant.

"It feels like something suspicious is going on," he said. Like I should know what Mom was doing on the lake, like maybe I *did* know. I didn't.

"I can't wait to get away from here," I said. My head hurt. I wanted to call Carlos and tell him about what I saw at the lake, but it seemed like an island problem. He was only thirty-seven miles away across the water, but it felt like four hundred.

"Yeah, that's cool." Ethan stood up and swiped the rest of his lunch back into his lunch bag. "Real nice, Fig." He flipped his chair closed and picked up his backpack. I only meant that I wanted to be anonymous, somewhere new. But by the time I got the words together, he was already up the ladder and gone.

CHAPTER 16

On Saturday morning, Izzy brought an apple pie, and I gave a silent thanks that it wasn't berry.

"My mom and I made this for you without ferns, I promise," she said.

"How did they turn out?"

"The fiddleheads cooked in garlic were much better, no contest," she said.

We dropped the pie off in the kitchen and went out back to the goat pen. Izzy wore too-big rubber boots and an even bigger flannel shirt, like she might need to clean the barn. Goats crowded around the gate when we squeezed through. Sometimes kids get scared around them, but Izzy crouched down and offered her fingers for sniffing. She laughed when they knocked her over.

"This is Margie." I helped Izzy back up. I held Fozzy back when Porridge squeezed around, sniffing my pocket for snacks. Other goats watched from the pole barn. Izzy made googly eyes at Margie and scratched behind her horns. We pulled carrot tops and chard from the garden, and Izzy fed them to Margie, Fozzy, and Speckles. I taught her how to use the currycomb, and we filled their water troughs. I tried to get them to play on the teeter-totter Mom built, but they wanted to lie around in the shade. Izzy liked finding eggs in the chicken coop too.

"I got lost on the way here," she said. "I asked a guy walking down the road in a cape and top hat for directions."

"Did he have a beard?"

"Yes. A gray beard."

"That's Ted," I said. "He's the closest magician. Did he do any tricks?"

She said he didn't, which is all right, because he's only average. We have the most magicians per capita of anywhere, according to the Murphy Council. They're getting a whole page in the class brochure. Wonderful Wayne floated Ethan's mom through a hoop at Ethan's eighth birthday party. I told Izzy about him, and about Dave, who works at the bookstore.

He makes paper moths out of old flyers. He sets them on the windowsill, and they fly around when someone opens the door, but he never tells how he does it.

After Izzy asked at least ten questions about the island, I said, "Do you want to just go to the museum?" I said it as a joke—it's one room—but she said yes. She looked so excited, we drove right over.

We looked at old resort pictures, preserved dead animals, costumed mannequins, and a dusty diorama of Truman Murphy and Marvelo. She studied the blurry Marvelo pictures.

"This could definitely be a dorsal fin," she said, and I walked away.

It took way longer than any of my previous trips, because she had so many questions. Ethan can't wait until next year, when he's old enough to volunteer to give tours. It might be one of the least interesting places on the island, but not to Ethan and Izzy. She wanted to try on one of the aluminum mermaid tails, but they keep them behind velvet ropes. She snuck closer, but the docent watched us.

"How did they move around in these?"

"I don't think they could," I said. She stared at the black-and-white pictures of girls in tails on the rocks in the cove. Tourists would take canoes out to see them, and the girls would splash and wave. The plaque read FROLICKING WILD MERMAIDS, 1911.

"What if they fell in the water? And where are the mer-dudes?" I'd never thought about it before, but she was right.

She wanted to know if they'd ever reopen the Ferris wheel, but it's pretty rusty. She studied costumes in glass cases and each of the pictures of the masquerade balls in the woods. Blurry masked faces danced in a circle of light from blazing candle chandeliers hung on wires between tree branches. It was as if they were in a magic bubble, or a snowglobe, and they could dance in the woods forever. Something about it reminded me of Mom on the lake.

"It's amazing they didn't burn the whole island down," I said.

We looked at costumes from the lion tamer and the fortune-tellers and watched old flickering movie clips of trapeze art-ists, contortionists, and other vaudeville performers. Izzy was so happy, it was like we were seeing the circus in real life.

"People think contortionists bend their spines, but spines are just joints and cartilage," she said. "They have to train their muscles to fold too. The bones just go where the body moves." Izzy said it like it was a totally normal thing to say. "I learned about spines after my mom hurt her back. Her doctor was cool. My questions didn't bug him." Izzy would have fit in on the island in the old days too. Even people who came just to work would end up performing, or sewing costumes, or making art. We read a bio of a hotel maid who became one of the best tightrope walkers in the world.

Every time the door opened, I checked for Mr. Mustard. I'd been looking for him everywhere—at the lake, at school, at the beach.

"I've been here before, but it's still great," Izzy said. "You okay?" She looked at me like she wanted to check for a fever. I wanted to tell her about my mom, but I didn't.

"It's been a weird week. There was a guy. I saw him on the ferry and again in the store the other day." I shrugged. "He creeped me out, like he was watching me."

"Yikes. What did he look like?" Izzy's voice rose.

"He has a yellow jacket," I said.

"Like a wasp?"

"No, mustard color. He's worn it both times I've seen him. I don't know his name, but I call him Mr. Mustard. It's like he wants something. Maybe he's looking for Huxley," I said, but Izzy didn't buy it. She had more questions, but I wanted to show her that I wasn't afraid, so I shrugged it off.

I wandered over to a big black-and-white picture of everyone who worked at the resort the summer of 1912.

"Were you related to any of these people?" Izzy looked at me with such wonder and awe, I wanted to say yes. My parents moved to Murphy before Carlos was born. Mom was going through a sculpting phase and liked the arty vibe of the town. Plus, houses were cheap. But there was nothing special about us. We wouldn't have fit in on Murphy back then any better than we do now. Izzy leaned into a diorama of the aviary. I bet she got good grades and did extra credit.

"Why aren't you in school right now?" I asked her.

She leaned out of the exhibit. "We got out for summer already."

The ancient museum docent cleared his throat right behind us and made me jump about a foot.

"Time for pie," I said.

Back at home, I parked by the barn, and we climbed up the rusty ladder and sat on top of the Rooster with half of Izzy's pie. It felt like a secret hideaway. We didn't talk while we ate, which was nice.

"You know your microscopic-bird idea?" I said. "I keep thinking about it. I have a new, also strange, theory. What if some, not all, obviously, but some of the birds you see flying around are ghosts?"

Izzy choked on a bite of piecrust and coughed. "What?"

"I mean, how would we know? They're up in the sky, and nobody looks that closely."

"I guess," she said. She chewed slowly, thinking.

"A lot of old resort animals stuck around, right? There's the group of wallabies in the woods. And my dad says giraffes grazed down the road when I was little. They shared a pasture with cows." She looked toward the trees like she could picture it. "We still have strange fish in the lake, and a few different exotic birds, and monkeys. Most people like it. Sometimes people say they see zebras, but they disappear. No one ever catches one or takes a picture." Izzy looked at me like she was waiting for a punchline. "So, the conclusion for some Murphers is that the zebras are ghosts."

"Maybe there are still wild ones," she said. "Like the library monkeys."

"You've seen the monkeys? It's a small island, and zebras are big. People would see them more often."

"Maybe only one is left, and it's good at hiding out. Maybe it doesn't want to get caught." I ate while she talked. "They thought jaguars were extinct in Arizona for years until they saw one on a motion camera. . . . What about Marvelo? Can we go find him? I can make another pie."

"My mom said a storm is coming." I was never going back to the lake. We watched Isadora and Buster stretch through the fence for chamomile weed. "And I might need to watch Leti if my parents are working. We're going to make cookies Thursday after school, though, if you want to come over."

"I'd like that. I think my mom is going to Lincoln." Izzy bit her lip. "Newt. I heard somebody talking at the pool."

"You like to eavesdrop."

"No! Well, yeah. Doesn't everybody?" Izzy adjusted the

barnacle shell she wore on a leather strap around her neck. It looked like a mini volcano.

"So?"

"Maybe I shouldn't say anything."

"What did you overhear at the pool?" I said. I wanted us to be the kind of friends who told each other everything.

"Never mind."

"Come on. You have to tell me now."

"I shouldn't have said anything." She blew her bangs out of her eyes. "It was about you. About what happened to your leg." I froze and Izzy leaned forward. "You passed by in your truck, and I guess the other people at the spring pool recognized you." Izzy watched me and I watched the grass wave in the breeze. It had been nice to have someone who didn't feel sorry for me. Izzy never asked how my leg felt. She didn't tilt her head and frown when she remembered. The top of the Rooster didn't feel like a cool hideout anymore.

I gave Izzy the short version and told her about my dreams.

"It's like I'm back there getting attacked all over again."

"How often?"

"Most nights. It's been a year. Maybe I would have forgotten about it by now. You know, without the dreams." But probably not. She had questions about the attack, and the bear, and the island, and how my family reacted, but talking about it made me feel like I was in different pieces. The leg piece took up most of the room, as usual.

"Want to hear something else strange?" I told her about what happened with Huxley and Ethan, Musky, Carlos, and Lyric's wishes. Once I started talking, I couldn't shut up.

"That's pretty peculiar," she said.

"My friend Ethan thinks it's magic. He wants me to take the bear to the Marvelo Festival, so that anybody who wants to can make a wish." He probably didn't want to go with me anymore. I made patterns in the pie syrup with my fork.

Izzy rolled her eyes. "It's definitely not magic. That stuff doesn't happen. Otherwise, someone could get a sausage on their nose." I didn't get it. "The old fairy tale? A couple gets three wishes from a tree sprite. The husband wastes the first wish on sausages. The wife gets mad and wishes a sausage was stuck to his nose. They have to use the last wish to get the sausage off. You never heard that?"

"I'm pretty sure you made it up right now," I said.

"It's a famous old story." Izzy laughed and for a minute she reminded me of my tía Carrie, who has my favorite laugh in the world. A bell rang from town. "What is that?"

I told her about the whale bell, how someone rings it if they see big whales in the channel or the cove. People walk over and look if they're nearby. Most of the time the whale is gone by the time people get to the water, but it helps to warn boats to be careful.

"A whale bell? That's the only thing it's used for?"

"Pretty much."

"I hope I get to ring it. There are twelve kinds of whales that swim near the island. I read that in the museum." She pulled her hair back into a ponytail. "But back to your bear. What did you wish for?"

"What would you wish for?"

"I wouldn't wish for anything, since it wouldn't work." She said it like she said how many whales there were, or how aye-ayes were endangered. Like it was another fact but a sad one.

"If it did work, if you had to wish," I said. It felt good to hear her say it wasn't magic.

"I'd wish to stay here. I could take care of Marvelo." She turned in the direction of the lake and sighed.

"He could take care of himself," I said, "*if* he was real."

"*She* probably can. She seems wily. It's more likely that some prehistoric creature has adapted to stay in this cool place than that a wooden bear can change what's going to happen. But still, what would you wish for?"

Telling her I would wish to leave the island right after she said she would wish to stay seemed rude. But I felt it pushing on my throat. It wanted to come out with all the other secrets

I had spilled. But a tiny part of me wanted to stay on top of the Rooster eating pie and for nothing to ever change.

The back door of the Rooster banged open and almost gave me a heart attack. Leti peeked over the edge of the roof.

"Leti! What were you doing in there?"

"Hanging out with that bear," she said. "He's funny-looking. Why would you keep a bear? Oh! What are you guys eating?"

"Stay out of my truck." I scowled at her.

"Is that your sister?" Izzy whispered, and I nodded. I didn't know if I felt more annoyed that Leti was in the Rooster without asking or that she was talking to Huxley. I was going to ignore her, but Izzy answered.

"We're eating pie. Do you want some?" Leti nodded and climbed up.

"This is my sister, Leti. And this is my friend Izzy."

"Did you make a wish on the bear?" Izzy asked.

"What?" Leti held her hand up to block the sun. She looked back and forth between Izzy and me.

"At least one of your brothers believes that that bear grants wishes," Izzy said.

"It does not," I said, but Leti was back inside the truck already. I pounded on the roof, and she hopped back out a minute later.

"Can I have some pie?" She smiled at Izzy the way she smiles at our dad when she wants something. It worked.

"Sure. There's more in the kitchen." Izzy nodded back toward the house.

"Did you make a wish?" I asked. Leti didn't answer, but she smirked over her shoulder as she skipped across the yard. Chickens ran toward her in case she dropped food. She shares her lunch with them. Sometimes she digs up nightcrawlers to feed to them like spaghetti. She'd probably give them pie too. Maybe she used a wish on money, or a basketball team at school, or to travel to see all her pen pals. She probably wished for pie. Unbelievable.

"Sorry about Little Leti."

"Why do you call her Little Leti? Is there another Leti?"

"In Lincoln," I said. "She's named after my aunt."

"Do people call her Big Leti?"

"Not that I've ever heard."

"If Leti is the only Leti on Murphy, why can't she just be Leti?" Izzy said.

"Sometimes she is, like at school, but mostly she's not," I said. "It's like you have to be different people in different places. Carlos is Carlos to the family, but his real first name is Eduardo, so a lot of his friends from school and the army call him Eddie. Leti even dresses different when we visit my grandma. Fancier. Nobody asks her to, but they expect it. Me too, but not as much."

"One kid can sure be a lot of people," Izzy said. She lay down like just thinking about it was heavy.

"Did you see that?" I said.

"What?" She looked around, and I pointed at the sky.

"Ghost birds."

"I can't see them through all the microbirds," she said. If anyone overheard us, they wouldn't have any idea what we were talking about, and that made it pretty great.

CHAPTER 17

Ethan accepted my apology when I showed up at his house the next day, sort of. He fit here, and I didn't. He would see it eventually.

"We're signing up for the festival," he said. "Right now. We can take the bear, give a short speech, and let everybody decide what they want to wish for. They can say it out loud. Or we can pass around slips of paper and those tiny pencils so they can write it down. We'll give the wishes to the bear."

"That's not how it worked, though. People tell Huxley their wishes."

"Who is Huxley?"

"The bear," I said. "I named him. What if something bad happens? What if somebody wishes for something awful?"

Ethan shook his head. "What if something fantastic happens? How about trusting people?"

"The bear-who-maybe-grants-wishes isn't an act. People will do tricks and play instruments. There might be wire walkers or sword swallowers. Everyone will be doing something."

"We can tell people that the bear might be magic," Ethan said.

"It still wouldn't be an act."

"We can make it good—better than juggling, synchronized dancing, or anything else we can learn in the week we have left. Word gets around. People might start showing up at your house once they learn about the bear. This way, we can get it all taken care of from the get-go. It's a phenomenon! You can hide him after, or whatever." Mom would freak out if people knocked on the door all the time to make wishes.

"We can tell them a mysterious bear with magical powers will be appearing at the festival," Ethan said. "For one night, and one night only, they can get what they want."

"Everybody? How long is our set?" I sat down like my knee wasn't killing me, but Ethan still noticed and asked if I needed anything. The festival would be different, and it might be awful, but at least Ethan wouldn't be mad. "What if we had a contest, for just a couple of people to get their wish?"

He frowned. "That's not as fun. Odds are, it's not gonna

happen right there onstage. We could add juggling or something else, a combo act. Do you still have your top hat or
your mom's unicycle?" They were in the attic with the squirrels. She put everything up there before my stitches were
even out.

"Are you worried about what your parents will say?" he
asked. His shoulders slumped, like it would be a deal breaker.

Me having a secret from them for a change—having a secret at all, when everybody knew every detail of my life—made
up for going back one more time. "It's fine. Let's do one big
wish. And then I won't have to juggle or wear a blindfold or
anything, right?"

Ethan wanted to come up with a backstory about the bear
to fill in the time for our slot at the festival. He wanted me to
wear a cape, but I definitely did not. He was smiling more than
he had in days, but I saw when he remembered, and his face
went blank.

"I don't understand why you want to move so bad. I know
you've been having a hard time, but this is home."

"Come on, Ethan. You know how things are. It will be better for everybody."

He shook his head. "It won't be better for me."

"I'll visit," I said. "Maybe my parents wouldn't be so
stressed. And they have a lot of cool new stuff there."

He argued, but Beth came out of the kitchen, and I *shush*ed him.

"Newton Gomez! Have you actually been driving a truck around the island? Without a license?" She put her hands on her hips, and I hung my head.

"I didn't tell her," Ethan said. "She saw you driving home from school."

"It was my parents' idea."

"Well, my house, my rules. When you have Ethan with you, you walk."

We left, and it was a relief to leave the truck parked in front of their house. Ethan hardly talked to me as we walked to the hall. He asked Gilda if they still had space, and she said they would always have space for us. She hugged me for a long time. I asked if she wanted to see Huxley, but she didn't need any details.

"I'll put you guys down as an animal act," she said. "Practice and make us proud. You only have a few days, but I want another high-quality production."

"It's going to be sensational," Ethan said. "It will be everyone's favorite act." Gilda laughed, like it was a joke.

Ethan jumped off the stage, and I took the stairs.

"Newt!" I spun around. Gilda stood between the old-timey footlights. "I'm so glad you're back."

"Just one more time," I said. Ethan kept walking.

"That's what I say every year," she called, and we left. I wanted to feel different somehow, but I just felt tired.

Dad got paid on Wednesday and came home with avocados, masa, chiles, and all the other stuff he picks up at the mercado in Lincoln because you can't find it on Murphy. I watched him line up limes, chiles, and onions in a row down the counter.

"Órale pues, there's a storm coming," he said. "You know what that means. We're going to need a lot of guac." Chuck barked outside like he could scare away the storm.

"Dad." I waited until he stopped mashing avocado and looked at me. "Why was Mom out on the lake? Does she do that a lot?" He mashed harder.

"I don't know everything your mom does," he said. "What's new with you? You want to have a party after school gets out Friday? The end of sixth grade! Let's celebrate! I'll make some steaks. What do you want?" I threw the avocado skins and pits in the compost.

"Steaks would be great. Thank you." I took a deep breath. "Next year maybe I could stay in your old room at abuela's, since I'm going to Lincoln Bay." He squeezed a lime half until it folded on itself.

"Your mom told me you asked about that. Murphy is your home."

"Sometimes it doesn't feel like it." My voice cracked. He probably thought I was a whiny little kid, but I had to keep going. "It might be better if I was gone."

"No es cierto, mijo. Your mom needs you. Your sister too. And me, I need you."

It wasn't true. It was so far from true, I wanted to cry. I rubbed my face and tried to shake it off.

"Newton. I hate to see you like this. Don't worry about us, mijo. Ever. Just keep getting yourself better. That's all we want. Is there something else bothering you?" I couldn't look at him. I couldn't add one more thing to the worry he already had to carry. All the extra problems because of me. I stared at the fruit bowl on the table and shook my head. They didn't understand.

He finished the guacamole and hugged me, but it didn't help. He rubbed my back.

"Don't worry so much. You're getting too skinny, man. Here, have a snack." He made me a little bowl of guac and chips before heading to town to settle our tab at Herb's. I took it outside. I like to sit on the porch behind the jasmine vines like it's a hiding spot. Margie and Chuck figure out where I am, even faster when I have food, but nobody else looks for me there. If Little Leti found me, she'd double-dip the chips.

The jasmine reminds me of my grandma Belinda's house in California. Everyone sits on the porch at night to cool off and tell stories. If our big family stories had a smell, it would be jasmine. Nobody sits on our front porch for stories. Maybe Mom tells stories to the crows. She must like remembering too, because she planted the jasmine. It's super scraggly and hardly ever blooms, but it tries.

I crunched chips and looked for ghost birds. Chuck emptied his kibble bowl, and the goats played on their plastic baby slide. The chickens scratched through the grass, looking for bugs around Dad's empty parking spot. The clouds got lower, covering the jasmine smell with the heavy metallic smell that comes before rain.

I could wish to leave Murphy right now and get it over with. Nothing was stopping me. There'd be a new me without any island problems. Wishing on the bear worked for other people. It would work for me too. Everything would be perfect. I rubbed the goose bumps on my arms.

I would miss people, but I could visit. And Izzy probably lived in Lincoln anyway.

The rain splattered the grass with tiny drops. The chickens and goats ran back to the barn. I wanted to make my wish before the storm got worse. Before Mom came out of the barn and Dad got home. Before I wimped out. I carried my empty bowls inside and grabbed the rabbit's-foot keys. It was finally happening. I could change everything. I floated toward the door. My face felt tingly. Chuck snuck inside when I opened the door, already stinking like wet fur. I looked around the yard, and all my happy feelings drained away.

The Rooster was gone.

CHAPTER 18

I woke up late the next morning. School was canceled because of the storm, and there was only one day left until summer vacation. Dad stuck a note on the fridge: Leti and I should take our jackets if we went out, and stay off the beaches. He drew a tiny sailboat in the trough between two fighting waves. The ferry was docked in Lincoln harbor, so my dad couldn't go to work. Captain Brian reported thirty-foot swells. Dad had gone out to help sandbag the marina to try to keep the streets from flooding.

Leti and I looked out the window, like we'd be able to watch the roiling sea through the trees. Rain *thunk*ed the window, and thunder shook the roof. Squirrels scurried to wherever they hid in the eaves. Leti left to watch something with explosions on TV, but I stayed and waited for lightning. Wind pushed through the cracks around the windows until the smell of seaweed and mud filled the house. Mom brewed coffee and made cocoa like my abuela does, whisking warm milk in a big pot over chocolate and cinnamon sticks. When I'd told Mom the Rooster was gone, she said we'd talk about it later. We had to deal with the storm first.

"If you stayed at Murphy School next year, we wouldn't have to worry about problems with the ferry in bad weather."

"I'm not staying at Murphy School, though. I'm going to Lincoln Bay," I said. She just lined thermoses up beside the stove like it wasn't even worth talking about.

The whale bell clanged over and over. I pictured the whales playing in the tall waves.

"Do they come closer to the island when the weather is bad?" I asked. She stared at me.

"Oh, the bell. They use it for emergencies too. It means the water is rising over the seawalls and everyone should move inland. Even higher than a king tide."

The sound faded in and out. "I can't hear it anymore," I said.

"The wind is blowing the other way. As long as they hear it around the coves." White light filled the kitchen, everything paused, and thunder came like a punch. Chuck knocked chairs over to squeeze under the table.

"What if somebody is there who doesn't know what the bell means?" I asked. What if Izzy heard the bell and went looking for whales?

"There aren't many tourists on a Thursday like this," Mom said. She pulled blankets out of the cupboard and stacked them on a kitchen chair. I watched our goats cluster together under the oak tree. Once Margie got enough rain, she would lead the way to the barn through the floppy plastic strips Dad had hung to keep out the cold, like a car wash for goats.

"I have a friend down there."

"Well, his parents will tell him."

"Her. Her mom's in Lincoln today."

"They wouldn't leave her behind. They probably told her about the bell." She poured coffee and cocoa into thermoses and tucked them around quilts inside an old apple box. More lightning, like someone snapped a picture of us. Izzy could be alone at the beach or wandering around the woods. Mom took a red-and-purple quilt from the top of the stack and spread it out over the table.

"A couple of days ago, I told her the bell was only for whales. I forgot about storms. Maybe we can drive over and check? She could be in danger if she doesn't know how fast the water can come." A wave could swallow a whole beach in seconds, tossing around giant bleached logs like rubber ducks in a bath. "Please? If you drive me over there, I can make sure she's all right before it gets too bad." I didn't look right at her, but I watched her hands. She stopped refolding the quilt and laid her hands flat on top, palms down, as if to keep it from floating away. You can know what someone will say and still feel disappointed when it comes out of their mouth.

"I bet she's fine. I've got to get some warm drinks down to the people helping in the marina." Her eyes were wide. She added the quilt back to the stack.

"Please, Mom? She could be in real trouble," I said.

"No, Newton. It's not safe out there. Stay put." She pulled on her windbreaker and picked up the box. "I'll be back soon. I'm taking Leti to help. Stay here in case your dad calls." She clomped down the hallway in her mud boots. The front door opened and closed, and the house was quiet.

I grabbed a jacket and rain boots and shoved two squished-up granola bars into my pocket. My parents' cars were gone. I could walk or not go at all, but I had a big piece of granite in my gut that wouldn't go away until I knew Izzy was safe. I checked that the goats had all made it into the barn and headed down the road. It would be quicker to follow the coast, but there would be no cover from rain, and no hope if a surge climbed up the beach. People died that way.

I slipped and fell twice in the driveway. My knee ached before I even got to the forest. I followed the trail between trees whipping and swaying in the wind like seaweed in the surf. Jeans helped some with the nettles and brambles, but they soaked up rain and mud.

And the rain came in blasts. Storm clouds pushed over trees like battleships, declaring war on Murphy. A pink flash of lightning lit an arrow to the beach. I sang a song instead of counting the seconds for thunder.

Fishermen and charter captains call the water lumpy if there are whitecaps, as if it were all a big bowl of undercooked oatmeal. I don't even know what they would call this. Nobody would go out on the ocean today. Someone's empty dinghy sloshed up and down the waves, its broken rope splitting the foam. Fallen branches littered the beach.

The rain stung my eyes. I followed a fence under humming power lines. I climbed over fallen trees. They stunk like turned dirt, and I couldn't help but think how much Ethan would want to poke around for anything interesting the roots might have pulled up. The wind howled like La Llorona crying for her lost children.

I could barely make out the bridge to Haven Cove through the gray light. My knee throbbed with each step. Water boiled under the bridge. Halfway across, a wave hit the beam and sprayed salt water straight up my nose. I coughed and gagged. You couldn't tell where the sky stopped and the sea started.

There was a nothingness, so I focused on the land. The whole row of cottages stood dark, power out, happy seaside colors dulled by gloom. A blue bucket rolled over the crest of a wave, pulled off someone's deck. Crab pot buoys dragged over the waves, probably spinning cages full of crabs below like carnival rides.

I passed two dark, shuttered, lifeless cottages. Peg and Jim Watson lived in the third. My knuckles stung with cold when I knocked on their door. I waited with my hand inside my shirt, but no one came. I made a fist and knocked louder. Maybe they couldn't hear over the rain and wind, but the house felt empty. I pounded one more time.

"Izzy? Izzy! Are you there?" I cupped my hands around my mouth and yelled toward the edge of the door. Wind made the cottage windows hum. Thunder rolled and cracked, so I leaned closer. "Mrs. Watson? Mr. Watson? The bridge is getting water!" I knocked more, but nobody answered.

I opened the side gate to check the back. I called hello over and over. Water lapped around garden beds up to the deck. I jumped up on a bare wooden block where something had already been washed away and looked around. A dark shape poked through the foam farther out in the waves. Izzy drowned, I thought, and the idea of it twisted around my ribs and squeezed like a bramble. I waded toward it. The water felt like sandpaper. I jumped to avoid another wave. If I stood on my tiptoes, most of the water stayed below my waist. I kept my mouth closed, but my teeth chattered. I stared until the dark shape rose on a swell. Not hair, but a fin or a flipper, rubbery and smooth. Something alive, cutting through the chop. Another wave swelled, and it was gone.

CHAPTER 19

While I knocked at the Watsons' cottage, storm water had risen under the bridge slats. Each wave made my leg a pincushion as I held on to the bridge with both hands. In one of Dad's stories, Marvelo and Manxadon rescued people from a falling bridge. I could use them now. Seeing each wave coming didn't make it any easier. I closed my eyes, stepped, slid my hands, and stepped again. Over and over. There was an orange glow, and I snuck a look—a passing car's headlights—and shut my eyes again. I imagined my parents pulling up in the truck. Mom would jump out with Dad's rain slicker held over her head and gesture for me to come get into the warm seat. They would bring towels, or even that purple quilt, and dry clothes. They would laugh at the storm and say something about the sky and sea fighting over our tiny island. My parents would drive me home with the heat blasting on high.

"What are you doing there?"

It wasn't my mom or my dad. A man's voice. "Are you all right?"

I opened my eyes, but headlights backlit the man standing at the edge of the bridge. The passenger door opened.

"Come on over here, son. Get off that bridge!" The man gestured. I held the rail until I reached the squish of land on the other side. Out of the water, my leg burned. I felt all the raindrops. All the sand pushed under my jeans. I walked in cement shoes. It was Mr. Watson from the bakery.

"Oh, hi," I said, like I was out for a walk.

"Newton, isn't it?" Mrs. Watson called from the car. I tried to smile, but my teeth knocked together. "He comes into the bakery, Jim. He's Robert and Vivian's boy." Mr. Watson looked back at her and paused.

"Come on, Newton. Let's get out of this weather." He led me to the car, and I climbed into the back seat. Mr. Watson sat in the front. We all looked out the windshield through the wipers at the water pouring over the bridge. "Some storm! Let's get you home, son. What were you doing out here, anyway?"

"I was coming to your house, actually," I said. Mrs. Watson smiled back at me as Mr. Watson turned the car around and headed away from the cove up the hill. "I'm sorry about the storm. Do you have somewhere safe to stay?"

"The town offered us cove people free rooms at the inn. There aren't many visitors on the island tonight." The car slowed around giant puddles and fallen branches.

"I appreciate the ride," I said. "Thank you."

"Why were you coming to our house, Newton?" Mr. Watson caught my eye in the rearview mirror. Mrs. Watson turned in her seat.

"I was looking for your niece Izzy. Is she at the inn?" I asked. Mrs. Watson frowned. "Is there something wrong? Is she still back at your house?" I swiveled around, but it was all darkness and water in the red glow of taillights.

"Newton, we don't have any houseguests right now. Our niece is Amber, and she's at college in New York. Her mom is home in Salem. Maybe someone else in the cove?"

"What? No. Izzy. She's my age. Sometimes she has crabs in her hair."

Nobody said anything until Mr. Watson cleared his throat. "Let's get you home, Newt, and we can talk to your parents about your friend, okay?"

"I met her on the beach a few weeks ago. We've talked a bunch of times. She likes to read a lot."

Mrs. Watson reached back and put her hand on my knee. It felt like a warm balm, but I saw when she remembered. She took her hand off, like it might hurt me. It wasn't even the right leg.

"I'm sorry, Newt. You must have it mixed up. We don't have houseguests, and I haven't seen a girl with a crab on her head. Have you, Jim?" He shook his head hard enough to make his jowls jiggle before she even finished talking.

"Not on her head," I said. "She puts shells from little ones on hair clips." I could tell it didn't make a difference. "She said she was . . ." I started to say Izzy had told me she was staying with the Watsons, but I couldn't remember if she had.

"Well." Mr. Watson changed the radio from a weather report to cello music. "There's nobody else in the cove right now. I'm sure she's at the inn. Would you like to take a quick look-see before we get you home?"

"His folks are probably worried sick," Mrs. Watson said. "Let's get him home and we can have his friend call from the hotel." I didn't want to tell them my parents were in the marina. With any luck, I could get home before them and they wouldn't know I'd been gone.

"What's her last name? We can ask Adrian at the front desk," Mrs. Watson said.

"It's . . . I don't know. I thought it was Watson, I guess." My cheeks felt hot.

Mr. Watson cleared his throat again. "We'll get it straightened out."

The Watsons worried when they didn't see any cars in our driveway, but I tried not to show how relieved I felt. I said they probably parked in the barn to get the cars out of the storm. Mrs. Watson asked me to double-check and wave from the window if there was someone home. Otherwise I could drive into town with them. They said they would have Izzy call, and pulled around to light the way to the door.

All the warmth I had soaked up in the car leaked out on the path to the house. Lightning flashed again, but I beat the thunder inside. The house smelled like burnt candles and coffee. I took off my boots and jacket and waited a few beats before I pulled back the curtain and waved. The car turned around and drove back into the storm.

CHAPTER 20

I slept without dreams for days. I'd wake up, not feeling scared, and fall straight back into emptiness. The storm caught me, my parents said, which is less getting caught out in the storm than feeling like the storm scooped out my chest. Water plunked through holes in the roof into bowls and buckets. Parrot squawks pierced my brain. Scratches from brambles and rocks I hadn't noticed striped my arms. My scars felt like the waves had split my leg open all over again, and my fingers kept needing to find them smooth and whole.

I missed the last day of school. I missed my weekend with Carlos too. Sixth grade was over. All year, I'd been thinking that when I left Murphy School, it would be dramatic. I would walk out the front doors and look back at the building, knowing I was done. Now it was over. I lay there, stuck and broken, like after the attack all over again.

Little Leti brought flowers from the teachers and told me about field day. She won the sponge relay and found the kindergarten class's gerbil by the compost bin in the garden.

"Don't worry about the goats," she whispered from the doorway. "I'm taking care of them for you. Margie likes me now."

"Of course she does," I croaked. "Thanks, boss."

"My pen pal in Texas has a sister who got into a bad car accident. I told her how sometimes it can feel like her sister is getting all the attention, but it will get better." Leti ran her toe along the floor trim and didn't look at me. "And it helps make everybody feel better to play games and stuff where you don't have to move around like we did."

"That's good advice, Let. You're a pretty great sister. The games did help." I never really thought about what it was like for her when I was hurt. I acted like I was doing her a favor by playing cards, even when I didn't have a lot of choices. I squeezed her hand and promised myself I'd do better. Mom brought me medicine and bitter tea. They left and I slept.

Dad wanted to take me to the doctor, but I begged him not to do it. He left to help find people's boats, trash cans, and patio furniture that the waves and wind had moved around. Mom called the doctor anyway, and she said it would be fine as long as my fever stayed under 105. It stuck at 103 for two days. Blurs of people paused in my doorway, like shadows of fish in the lake.

"Dad," I said, "the truck is gone. Somebody stole it."

"I know, mijo. Don't worry about that now. I brought you some soup."

"I'm sorry about the truck, Dad." He shushed me again and spoon-fed me black bean broth. He said it was his magic potion to cure illness. It looked like inky witch's brew.

"This reminds me of feeding you after you came home from the hospital last year." He let out a shaky breath. "I was so scared, Newt. I watched you sleep, like when you were a baby. I had to make sure you were breathing, even when we knew you'd be all right. We could have lost you." He sniffed and wiped his eyes. Dad never talked about it. "I'm sorry, I shouldn't have brought it up."

"It's okay to talk about it. I mean, I don't mind. It seems like it helps," I said, and he squeezed my hand through the blanket. "Thanks, Dad. For everything, I mean." He held my hand until I conked out again.

The parrots stayed in the cherry tree day and night, mostly quiet.

Carlos brought comics and pan dulce and moved the little TV from the garage to my bedroom so we could watch movies.

"Why didn't you move back after the army?" I asked Carlos. He thought about it.

"I don't know. I went to Lincoln U., and that felt like home too."

"Do you like your new promotion?" I yawned, but I really wanted to hear about it.

"It's pretty great, yeah. I'm working a lot of hours, but we're setting up this new program for downtown restaurants to compost their food waste instead of sending it to the dump. I feel like I'm making a difference, and it's nice to have some extra money. I don't worry about my student loans so much. If you want to go see Dr. Wu again, I can probably swing it."

"You'd do that?" My chest hurt when he smiled at me.

"Anything you need, Figgy." He squeezed my foot. "Monsters or aliens?" I knew I must be in bad shape to get to pick the movie. We watched *Godzilla*. Leti sat on the floor with Carlos and drew new monsters to send to her Scottish pen pal. I fell asleep before the end of the movie.

"Are you busy?" Mom stood in the doorway in her work clothes. I could feel sunshine on my legs like a spotlight on the scars, but I didn't pull the covers up. She moved closer, and I smelled roasted chiles and vanilla. "I want to teach you something. Try to keep an open mind."

She sat down on my bed and talked about being in labor before Carlos was born. It took two days, and it was horrible. She spent almost her whole pregnancy with me worried about going through it again. A friend taught her to think about pain like riding a wave.

"Instead of getting overwhelmed, you accept that it's there and ride it like a surfer," she said. "Your birth was much easier."

"Why are you telling me this?" I rubbed my face.

"Because once I thought about it that way, it hurt less. You and Little Leti were a piece of cake. Relatively. I'm telling you because it can help you."

"I'm not having a baby."

"No, but you could use it for your dreams. Or when you feel crummy. Accept the pain, or fear, and ride it out. Like it's a wave and you're floating. Or you're a bird, and you can fly over the crest until it's safe to land again." I didn't say anything, so she headed for my door.

"Do you know what my dreams are like?" I asked. I didn't think she would answer, but she shook her head. "They're like being attacked, every night. I smell dirt and blood. My blood. I feel the teeth." She stood in the doorway between me and the rest of the house, holding the frame, like she could keep my dreams there in my room. But I was there too. "I'm pretty tired. I accept the need for a nap. I'm going to ride the wave to sleep." She took something out of her pocket and set it on the table next to my water bottle.

A heart milagro on a leather strand.

CHAPTER 21

Dad knocked on my door.

"You've got company, Newt. You up to it, mijo?" I sat up.

"Is it a girl?"

"No, it's Ethan. Want me to send him up?"

"Sure. How come you're not at work?"

"I took a couple days off." Dad never takes a day off that's not a day off for everybody, ever. He goes to work on Christmas Eve, but he's home in time for tamales. "I'll get Ethan. This is the third time he's been here, by the way, but your mom wanted you to rest."

I took a drink of water and rubbed the duvet over my teeth. I couldn't remember the last time I brushed them, but ever since the storm, I'd been drinking a lot of water. Ethan ran up the stairs, with Boxwood's toenails tapping behind him.

"Hey, you okay? Dude, you look wrecked. What happened? I heard somebody found you, like, trying to drown yourself on the cove bridge!"

I shook my head.

Ethan brought grapes and toast and sat down on the beanbag in the corner to watch me eat. "I've been coming over twice a day. Rocket came a couple times too, but they had you quarantined. I can't believe you missed the end of sixth grade! Where's the truck? I didn't see it outside."

I sat up, swallowed, and told him about the Rooster.

"What? Did you leave it unlocked?"

"I don't think so."

"Who would take it?" Ethan asked. I leaned back into my pillows and sighed. "Somebody had to know Huxley was magic."

"Why take the whole truck, why not just Huxley?" I asked.

"Because he's ridiculously heavy . . . and magic?" Ethan lined up grapes, but he couldn't help smiling. He wanted me to say it so badly.

I sighed. "Why me? What's with me and bears?" I didn't want to talk about Huxley, so I told him about my dreams and Dr. Wu. No matter what kind of bad luck I had, Ethan had worse luck losing his dad. I didn't want to bother him, but the storm washed away my resistance.

"My mom took me to therapy after my dad's heart attack," Ethan said. "It was a group of kids who'd lost a parent. One guy was there because his cat died."

"Did it help?"

"Maybe? Yeah, probably. My dad collected coins when he was a kid. After . . . I kept finding old coins. More than usual. It seemed like more than a coincidence. Looking for them makes me feel better." He picked up some shoes and threw them in my closet. "What were you doing on that bridge? You missed field day, and the festival rehearsal. I went. It's just the usual, testing lights and stuff. You remember. They think we're trying to be mysterious, since you and the bear weren't there."

"We're going to have to cancel," I said. Ethan jumped up.

"No way!" He paced around my room. "We've got three days. We can find him."

"Yeah, right."

"I'm serious. What are we going to do?" He looked at me like I could have the answer. "What about that girl? Izzy? She can help." I laughed. It was the loudest sound I'd made in a week.

"I don't think she can help us. She was just some tourist

playing a weird game." I told him about the Watsons. Boxwood and Chuck played tug-of-war with a dirty sock.

"Newt. Don't take this the wrong way, but is there any chance you made this girl up? You've been under a lot of stress lately, not sleeping and stuff. Maybe she's a ghost! That would be amazing!"

"No, but—" I remembered and sat up. "Leti talked to her. I didn't make her up."

"Where would she be? If she was real, I mean." Ethan looked at me with pity, like that proved his point.

He gasped. "She took the truck!" He wiped a hand over his face, as if the dust from a magic bear, a missing girl, and a sick friend tickled his nose. The goats bleated out in the field.

I had a feeling I knew who took the truck, but it wasn't Izzy. It was Mr. Mustard.

"Do you see the wrinkles on their paws?" Ethan pointed to Boxwood's back foot. "Maybe there's dog palm reading. If you can read people's palms by the wrinkles, why not dogs'? We could do that for the festival."

"They don't even have lines like people do."

"They have, like, cracks, and tiny lines. We could tell their fortunes. All the dogs on Murphy could know their future." He inspected Boxwood's front paw. "What will we do if we can't find the bear? We told people there would be a bear."

"You told people," I said.

I wanted the truck back. I wanted Huxley back.

It took half an hour of me refusing to do any magic, contorting, fireworks, singing, or juggling for us to come up with one doable but still terrible plan B. Ethan gave me a hug even though I stank, which he didn't even mention. Carlos came to check on us, and Ethan and Boxwood left.

"How you doing, baby bro?"

"Hey, you're back."

"You bet! I couldn't let you keep getting all this attention. Abuela is downstairs. She asked me for a ride over."

I sat up and swung my legs over the side of the bed. "Why?"

"She wanted to see you, silly. It's a family reunion downstairs. Come down."

Abuela stood in the kitchen at the stove beside Dad, stirring something in a pot. She hugged me over and over. "Siéntate, mijo. I made you a snack."

I sat down and ate fideo. Each chewy little clump of orange noodles was a power-up. She didn't sit down. She stood up straight and cleaned, even behind the jars and canisters. She stacked food from grocery bags along the counter. I think she liked cooking here, as long as no goats came inside. She made a pot roast and fresh bread, even though it was hours until dinner and she said she wasn't staying that long. Mom and

Dad drank coffee and showed her where to find things, but she wouldn't let them help. Little Leti and Carlos pigged out, but I felt full after a few bites.

"When you come to stay with me, we'll fatten you up," my grandma said. She took my plate and winked. I looked at my parents.

"Newt," Mom said, "your abuela says that if you really want to, you can try staying with her for summer break."

"I want you to come stay with me, if that's what you really want," abuela said. She finally sat down. "We could cook together, and there are other kids nearby, you know. Javi could show you around Lincoln Bay."

"That sounds great." I must have been in shock.

Before abuela and Carlos left, Mom gave them goat-milk soap and lotion. Abuela wasn't going to go hug a goat or anything, but when she hugged me goodbye she said she liked the mint smell.

I headed back to bed, but Dad wanted to talk.

"Even though Deputy Pat knew about the truck, I can't call the police or anything, since it wasn't registered. Sorry, mijo. But you want to stay with your abuela this summer?" He squeezed my arm. I nodded. I had hoped my parents and grandma would say yes, but now that they had, I didn't feel like celebrating. It's not like things are always great on the mainland. My grandma's neighbor Martin is the grouchiest guy I know. My tías bicker a lot. And my friends wouldn't be there.

"Get some rest. We'll talk later," Dad said. Chuck followed me upstairs. Mom said he'd been trying to get to me every time he came in the house, but they blocked the stairs with a baby gate so he wouldn't wake me up. He's the big, furry family nurse.

I checked Chuck's paws for lines before I went to sleep, but the only thing I saw in his future was walking through more mud.

CHAPTER 22

Dad went back to work, so Leti must have let Izzy in. When I woke up, she was sitting on the floor, with Chuck asleep beside her. She sat straight and still, like she didn't want the floor to creak and wake me up, which was impossible. After the storm, the house groaned like a ship at sea.

I sat up. "My mom says it's good that the floors creak, because even the ghosts can't sneak up on you."

"You have the most unique house," Izzy said. I would've argued if I was more awake. There's a brother and sister at school with a slide built into the second-story wall between their bedrooms. I was jealous of them for ages.

"I went looking for you," I said. Izzy looked pale. Sticky shadows hung around her eyes. "During the storm, I mean. I didn't know if you knew that Haven Cove could flood. I worried I had made you up. You're not staying with the Watsons." I turned on my side to face her. "Who are you?"

"Still me," she said. "I didn't exactly lie about where I was staying—I just didn't tell you when you guessed wrong."

"Did you take my truck?"

"No, I'm too young to drive." I think she wanted me to laugh, but I didn't. "I was at another house in the cove, a couple down from the Watsons'."

"With who?"

"My mom," she said.

"Whose house is it?"

"Mine, sort of. It was my great-great-grandma's house when it was new. Truman Murphy built it for her. She was a magician at the resort, but her picture isn't in the museum. It should have been. She sewed the wildest costumes. Gertrude the Great?"

"Like Gertrude Lake?" I asked, and Izzy nodded. I'd never thought about how the lake got its name.

"My grandpa inherited the house, and we used to come visit in the summer. He taught me a lot about the woods and stuff, about finding mushrooms and berries." There is a periwinkle-blue house in the cove called the magician's cottage. I might have seen Izzy before and never noticed.

"She was one of the first female stage magicians. You know

what? She had an act with a bear for a while. It rode a bike or something!" She laughed. "You should come to the house and see the old pictures. She was really something."

"Where are your parents?"

"My mom was in Lincoln during the storm. She couldn't come back when they stopped the ferries. She's been going back and forth. My aunt broke her hip, and she's got some dementia, so my mom stays with her a lot."

"So you're here alone?"

Izzy shook her head.

"Only sometimes. My dad, he left us after Christmas. He's not a very good person. I got worried when you told me about Mr. Mustard. I thought it might be him looking for us. My mom wasn't here, so I hid."

"I'm sorry," I said. "That sounds really scary."

She pet Chuck's wrinkly jowls and didn't look up. "I saw the guy you were talking about. It wasn't my dad. Because of my aunt, my mom hasn't been able to work, and with him gone, money is really tight. When she's gone, I try to keep the house clean and find food so our groceries last." I pictured her in the woods with her basket. A parrot landed on the branch outside my window, but it didn't feel like the right time to tell her.

"You could go to your aunt's house with your mom," I said.

"She has a tiny apartment, and she doesn't like visitors. Or kids. I don't have fun staying here alone, if that's what you think. I'm always worried about getting caught, or someone thinking my mom isn't doing a good job. I'm not supposed to tell anyone when my mom's gone. She's trying to find extra help for my aunt so she can come back."

Izzy told me that she got old produce from the free trays at the Unity market and from the dumpster behind Herb's. Not half-eaten stuff, but food still in packages past the expiration date. She ate a lot of oysters for the protein. She didn't used to like them; she liked them for a while, and then she got sick of them. When she thought that Mr. Mustard might be her dad looking for her, and her mom was gone, she slept in a utility shed in the woods. She went back to the cove only if she needed to take a shower.

"Don't you get scared? Like at night, or during the storm?"

"I'm always scared," she said. She stopped playing with Chuck's fur and looked straight at me. "You're the only one I've told. It's a secret. Don't tell anybody, okay?"

I nodded. "Are you going to leave again? Where's the shed you're staying in? Do you need anything? I have a pretty good sleeping bag."

"It's okay, my mom's back. The storm freaked her out, and she says that she can't keep going back and forth. We might have to move to Lincoln. But I won't leave without saying goodbye. You're lucky this is your home. I wish I belonged here." I sat up and the parrot flew away.

"Sometimes life looks easier for other people, or somewhere else, but it doesn't mean it is. I'm the only kid on the island who's been attacked by a bear. Maybe the whole state. We're the only Mexicans. I'm the only one who drives a big silver truck, or used to." I swallowed. Everybody probably felt this way. "I'm just trying to say you're not alone."

Izzy nodded, but I don't think it made her feel any better. She said that her mom might get worried that she'd told me, so I promised not to say anything. If I needed to talk to her, I should leave a note inside the book on the lost kingdom of Niya at the library. There was only one book on Niya.

"Maybe your bear really is magic," Izzy said. "I would like it to be. Could I make a wish now, please?"

I had to tell her Huxley was gone. She curled up and closed her eyes, like she could freeze time until things got better. I brought her a glass of water, and Chuck lay down beside her.

After a while, I asked Izzy to help me make lunch for Leti. The cupboards were overflowing with my abuela's groceries. We pigged out on grilled cheese and soup. I felt hungrier than I had in ages.

Izzy didn't want to, but when she left, I made her take all the goat cheese, jam, frozen tamales, and leftover fried chicken she could carry.

If my regular dream was a tree with rough bark and sticky sap, the one I woke up from later that day was smooth gray driftwood. The same but different. I pictured the swell of a wave, and me floating on top. I listened to parrots and smelled grass and blossoms. I thought I heard a cartoon from the TV through the floorboards, but it was just Leti doing goofy voices.

I sat at my desk and wrote the dream down. I described the attack as it had happened, and I didn't leave anything out. When you don't go to school for a week, your hand gets lazy and cramps up when you try to write. I wrote anyway. I wrote five different endings that couldn't be terrifying. Puppies and laughing and everything floating away in little pieces like seafoam breaking on the surf. I wrote until I could barely move my fingers, and all the new dream endings had food. I went downstairs, one stair at a time. I looked at the house like it was the first time I had seen it. I ran my fingers over the cool, colorful walls.

Mom milked goats in the barn. Little Leti threw hoops out back. I couldn't remember hearing any dribbling while I was sick, but it was a regular morning again. I pictured my grandma at her house, watching telenovelas while something delicious baked in the oven.

After I ate two breakfasts, I called Musky to see if I could borrow something for the festival. He said to come pick it up, but without the Rooster, that meant walking.

Maybe it was because I was leaving, or because the grass had grown as tall as me in the last week, but it felt like I might be somewhere new. I tried to imagine what the island had been like before houses had Christmas lights and scrap metal sculptures and peace flags hanging off porch railings. It must have been fun to see wild animals and stilt walkers and all the other extraordinary things. I squinted at every puddle to spot a water bear, but I didn't see any.

I kept an eye out for Mr. Mustard. But since he probably stole the Rooster and Huxley, he wouldn't be lurking around. I should have known when he kept looking at me on the ferry and at Herb's that he was up to no good. I should have told Dad when Mr. Mustard gave me a dirty look as he drove by in that purple van.

I stopped.

I knew how to find him. When he drove past us on the ferry, his truck had a business name on the side. Something that started with *M,* with an owl with butterfly wings. I could find out whether he took the Rooster or not.

I called Ethan when I got back from Musky's.

"We should call the police," he said. I told him my dad said we shouldn't, and his sigh blasted through the phone. "All right. I guess. At least you know what happened, maybe."

"Or . . . we can try to get it back." It just came out. I felt awake and strong, better than I had since the storm. Since long before the storm.

"What?" Ethan said.

"I want to rescue the Rooster," I said. "Hang on."

I looked up antiques companies on the mainland on Mom's computer. I found it on the second page of results. Minerva Antiques & Oddities. That was it! No website. No reviews. Only eleven blocks from the docks.

Ethan didn't need as much convincing as he should have. He kept talking until I interrupted: "We'll make a plan."

"Maybe it shouldn't be only us. Your dad could help?"

"No, we can do it," I said. "And Izzy too." We hung up and I grabbed a piece of paper to write a note to stick in Izzy's book at the library. I could go alone, but it would be better with friends.

CHAPTER 23

I stood under the willow tree in the shadows. People moved in and out of the stage door. Most of them wore at least part of their costumes.

I told my mom and dad that Ethan and I were going to watch a movie at his house while Beth helped with the box office at the festival. Ethan and I had to practice.

I wasn't ready. I could tell Gilda that I didn't feel well enough yet. Anybody could wear the old bear suit I'd borrowed from Musky. It sat in the bag by my feet. But Ethan would be crushed. And a tiny, deep part of me remembered how much I loved the festival. Maybe, if things came together, it could be fun again. One last time before I said goodbye to Murphy.

I opened the door. Backstage smelled like dust, paint, and the cedar oil they used to clean the stage. It also smelled like sweat and kerosene from the fire dancers, the sharp tang of a metal frame holding octopus arms on a skirt, and the shoe polish on the archer's shiny boots. A backstage smells like practice and possibilities.

I soaked up everything, because it started to feel like it used to, when coming into the theater before a show would make me want to bounce off the walls, though it was different without my family. Dust thickened in the light beams over my head. Ethan stood behind me, dressed like a circus ringmaster. Top hat. Red satin jacket with tails. Fake mustache. Flip-flops. He smudged something dark around his shiny eyes, like he hadn't slept in weeks for mysterious reasons.

"Ready?" He'd been there all day, just waiting for the fun to start. Someday, Gilda would make him master of ceremonies. Murphy is his kingdom. I peeked through the stage curtain from my favorite spot by the ropes. Empty chairs and decorations made my breath shake. It's the same every year. The audience sat underneath one hundred different old lamps, bases bolted to the ceiling, lampshades secured, ready to dim and start the show. Big paper lanterns hung above the chairs too. The stage was empty except for a giant papier-mâché Marvelo with foil-covered cardboard scales. They built a new one every year.

This is what happens when a big group of wacky people do something together. It felt upside down and outrageous but nice, in a Murphy way. Ethan tapped my shoulder, and we headed to the lawn outside to rehearse. My heart beat like a drumroll. I put the bear suit on.

"It's hot in here," I said. Ethan leaned forward.

"What?" he said. I said it really loudly three times before he heard and understood. The costume head was a big sound muffler, so I took it off and we changed our plan again. I would be a fortune-teller bear. Ethan would act like he was the bear tamer and ask me questions that the audience asked him. I would give advice. Except nobody could hear anything I said, so I would mime something he could "interpret." He'd do most of the work, and I got to be the anonymous guy in the bear suit.

The audience lined up out front, and Gilda made us go backstage. People bring a lot of food to the festival. Tom-with-the-beard always makes a big pot of crab dip that everyone loves. Most people goofed around in the dressing rooms, but I stood by the curtain and watched the auditorium fill up. My hands were sweaty, and my body felt like it was humming. I could tell who was new by the way they looked around. The lights dimmed to a golden orange while people found their seats. The whole room swelled. I didn't see Izzy. Leti sat with her friend Ramona. I worried that my parents would come on a whim and see me there, and I'd have to explain, but I didn't see them either. I watched Herb and Arlene and some teachers sit down. Almost the whole island was there.

A band played old-fashioned music in the pit below the stage. A couple of older guys from school juggled glitter-covered sea stars. One of the ushers wore roller skates and a tutu. He spun in blurry circles down the aisle.

"Showtime, everybody!" Gilda passed by in a tiara with a headlamp. She checked off performers on her clipboard. I peeked around the curtain one more time to look for my parents. They probably would've come if I had asked, but it was like we had all decided to not talk about it anymore. I sat down behind the curtains on a giant clamshell built for a mermaid routine and took deep breaths.

Gilda stepped into the spotlight to wild applause. She talked about the history of vaudeville, like she does every year. She thanked everybody for coming and announced that festival proceeds would go toward storm relief. Performers would collect donations at intermission. The audience cheered even harder.

"And now, by the power of Marvelo, let the festival begin!"

It started with an aerialist on long green scarves. Next, a fireball-spitting sword swallower. Heat rolled backstage with each blast. The people in the front row seemed relieved when his act was over. A lady played "Somewhere Over the

Rainbow" with a bow on a saw. The fighting acrobats almost smashed Marvelo's tail. Gilda gave me a thumbs-up from the other side of the stage. I nodded and held the bear's head in my lap like a shield. Number five was the bubble man, who has been doing the show since I was little. He put volunteers inside giant, swirling bubbles. Then the big Marvelo chased colorful first graders dressed as cichlids. They got a standing ovation, and my hands got clammy. Number seven was a magician who made it snow and swept it all up with a broom he never touched. The crowd cheered louder after each act.

Ethan stood next to me. It was time for us to go on, but I didn't know how we could follow all that.

"We've totally got this, Fig," Ethan said. "We are festival pros. Follow my lead. Or, you know, put your own spin on it. Whatever. It's going to be great." He adjusted his tie and took a big breath. "Right?"

"Right."

Our set was six minutes long. I put my bear head on, and Ethan gave me a push. We stood under the stage lights between the papier-mâché Marvelo and the dark, lumpy audience. People say that something is like a dream when it's foggy and confusing, but to me, dreams are sharp and saturated, and real life is blurrier. The stage felt fuzzy. My heart beat a *whoosh*ing sound. I paced around Marvelo, trying to shake off feeling submerged. Ethan talked to the audience, and I couldn't hear anything. A few hands went up, and I figured out he called for volunteers. He listened. I tried to look like I listened too, but when he repeated the question for me and the audience, I heard, "Mmmmmgorp . . . fay . . . bitten . . . job or flibcan toll?"

Ethan raised his eyebrows and nodded. I couldn't tell if it was a yes or a no question, or if they wanted a longer answer. He stood there in his top hat with the microphone and waited. I realized too late that he had the easy part. I waved my arms, as if explaining something, and nodded and grunted as loud as I could. The drummer in the pit hit the snare drum. Ethan translated and made a face, as if he was apologizing for my brutal, bear honesty. I could hear the audience laugh through the *whoosh*ing. My heart beat fast enough to burn my chest, and more hands went up.

Ethan called on somebody else. I hammed it up and gave a couple of spins with my answer, lifting up one leg like a ballerina bear. Ethan nodded, rubbed his chin, and told the audience "Da bear bliffs clamtop soba!" They laughed again. If people knew it was me inside the suit, the weirdo kid who got bit by a bear and drove around with a bear, I couldn't know. We did seven more questions, more clapping and hands going up each time. I jumped, spun, and balanced on tiptoes, gesturing and grunting. Ethan hammed it up more and more. I growled and shook my head. A bear-wisdom bonanza.

When Ethan bowed, I bowed. People clapped and we bowed again. Pushing through the curtains was better than breaking the surface of the lake after a dive. I pulled the bear head off. I laughed the way you do when things aren't exactly funny, but they're better.

CHAPTER 24

The audience clapped a lot, and I don't think it was just to be polite. When you've performed enough, you can tell when they mean it. Backstage, people patted our shoulders and gave us the thumbs-up. A guy in a green cowboy hat walked toward the stage with giant marionettes, and just like that, our part was over. I gave the costume back to Musky and became Newt again. I drank cherry soda and ate cheese cubes and crackers. I couldn't get enough food.

"Good job, Newt!" Gilda smiled so wide. People I didn't even know asked how we'd thought of it and said they hoped we would do it again next year. Leti came backstage and gave me a hug.

"Abby and I are sleeping at Ramona's. We knew it was you

the whole time, but that just made it better." People high-fived and snapped pictures. At the festival, just for one night, we were all teammates in the middle of a game where everybody wins.

The mermaids rolled the clamshell away to get ready, so I stood and watched another magician, the octopus, a band, and a contortionist. There were only a couple of other kid acts. Gilda came out and made jokes while stagehands rigged a cable and spread blue-and-white fabric over the floor. I looked for Izzy again, but the audience was a dark forest. The first year, when we did our card trick, I told myself they were trees, and it was easy to believe.

Gilda left and the audience hushed. A giant crow with wide onyx-colored wings, a shiny bodysuit and tights, and a face-sized beak with a feathered headpiece climbed onto a wire tied across the stage. The crow faced the audience, and the violinist in the band played music that sounded as if the song itself was trying to balance on a wire. A stagehand turned on a fan, and the fabric rippled across the stage to become clouds and sky. The crow lay down across the wire and spread its enormous wings. The hall hushed, except for the violin. The crow tilted to one side and the other, as if flying through the currents of a fabric sky. Goose bumps covered my arms, even though backstage was a million degrees. The crow lifted its head to turn its beak to the other side of the wire. The light caught its neck, and I froze.

The costume covered almost everything, but I saw it: a purple ribbon with four milagros. I couldn't see what they were, but I knew: a truck, a goat, a boy, and a flaming heart. She turned, and the D.S. tattoo at the base of her right thumb rode over an imagined current. The crow was my mom.

The performance was flawless. Her best ever. Even though she didn't sweep snow or swing fire like the big hits of the first half of the show, the audience stood and cheered. Mom curtsied and hopped down from the wire. She ran right past me.

"Mom!" I said, but it got lost in the brush of her wings against Marvelo. "Vivian, wait!" The curtains fanned over me, and she was gone.

I looked for her but only found one glittery black feather on the props table. Ethan juggled stars outside. "Did you see her?" I asked, but he hadn't.

For the rest of the show, I stayed by Ethan and the jugglers near the backstage door. I hoped to catch my mom, but there was no sign of her or the black wings. Gilda called us inside when it was over, and we all crowded on the stage to take our bows. Without the bear costume, the stage lights felt like sunshine. All the houselights, every lamp and lantern, shone brightly. The band kept playing. People stood around like they didn't want to leave. I didn't either. Everything I loved about the festival ran from the stage boards under my feet to the rafters. I whispered an apology for forgetting how amazing it is. I took deep breaths of each magical speck of festival dust. Trying to memorize everything was like trying to cup water in my hands. I'd almost missed the whole thing.

Izzy came toward the band pit, a salmon swimming against the current. I bent down to the edge of the stage.

"You were magnificent!" she said.

Somebody finally turned off the bright stage lights, but I still felt warm. I wanted to ask Izzy if she saw my mom, but she'd never met her.

"Do you want to go to a party?" I said instead. I was planning to skip the wrap party, but she said yes. We followed the parade of people under supernova lights on the lake path to the café. Ethan still wore his whole costume, even the top hat, and offered people unsolicited advice.

Mom wasn't at the party either. I looked for Gilda. She must have known, but she hadn't told me.

I wanted to dream about the show. Maybe in a dream my brain would show the parts I'd missed, the way it did with nightmares. Somebody asked if I was the bear guy, and I said yeah. I didn't know if they meant the show, the attack, or Huxley. I led Izzy over to meet Ethan.

"What did you tell him about me?" she said. I remembered how we'd talked about her hair crabs and nettles, and how she could be a fugitive.

"I told him that you're my friend." We got a slice of cake. "And maybe you're imaginary." Ethan stood with a dancer and a couple of aerialists.

"This is my friend Izzy," I said. "Izzy, this is my friend Ethan." Ethan raised his eyebrows.

"Fig didn't make you up!"

"He didn't make you up either." She eyed him. "I know about the bear. Newt left me a note," Izzy said.

I felt my face get warm. I leaned toward them. "I think we should make our plan to get Huxley back." We took even more cake to the lake gazebo and talked about all the ridiculous ways we could get Huxley and the Rooster back. Izzy watched the water like she thought Marvelo might jump out.

"You're not going to see anything over there," I said. Izzy laughed, but she still faced the lake. "We could offer to buy it back from him? Like a Rooster ransom?"

"Do you have any money?" Izzy asked. I did not.

"I could get my coins," Ethan said. I laughed, but he didn't. It was hard to see in the dark, but he looked serious. "My 1913 buffalo nickel, the 1909 penny, and my 1982 No P Roosevelt dimes. You can have them all. Mr. Mustard might take a trade for the coins. Antiques stores buy coins! Or we could sell them for the money and offer that to him."

A group of people left the café in a burst of noise. One guy did cartwheels, and somebody played a trombone.

"I can't take your coins, Ethan," I said. "Thank you. I don't think he would take money even if we had it. He wants Huxley. You can't put a price on that." I kept an eye on the paddleboats for any moms or crows.

"We could steal it," Izzy said. "You didn't leave the keys inside, did you? Wait. Did you?" They looked at me. I told them the keys were home under the Guadalupe statue by the front door. The rabbit's foot was like a furry cushion for her feet.

"There you go," Izzy said. "We don't even need to hot-wire it. That's where they always have trouble in the movies. But you have the keys. You know where it is. Let's go get it!" It seemed easier than bartering with coins. But still, really stupid and dangerous.

"I don't know," I said. "That guy—"

"What do we know about this guy, Newt?" she said.

"Nothing," I said. "But all we'd have to do is drive it away. Except it's in Lincoln. I've never driven there because, you know, normal laws."

"It's up to you," Izzy said. More laughter leaked out of the party, and the lake lapped the shore.

"I've got to go," I said. Any plan would be risky. For now, we all went in different directions.

The rain smelled like oysters, tree bark, cement, and seagrass. Izzy wouldn't let me walk her back to the cove, and Ethan's mom was at the party, so he stayed. I took the long way home, around the lake under drizzle and supernova lights.

Maybe Mom would still have her wings when I got home. She might talk about the plate spinner or the mermaid I missed. She could say something about our act.

Walking alone in the dark freaked me out, but I kept going until I saw the warm light spilling out of our windows. Dad slept in front of the TV. Mom sat in the kitchen, drinking tea. She didn't have wings. She wore a green hoodie and yoga pants.

"Where'd you come from?" she said. I could've lied, even if everybody in town said they saw me there, but I didn't.

"The festival," I said. "I went to the festival." She studied me and twisted her mug over the tabletop. It left wet, broken circles over the surface.

"I thought you were going to Ethan's," she said.

I shrugged. "I lied." I thought I'd feel guilty, but she had so many secrets lately, I didn't. She pulled her knees up inside the hoodie.

"How was the show?"

I felt like I was looking down at us, as if we were a diorama in the Murphy Museum, or a tide pool. I watched her play with the milagros on her ribbon and held my words in my mouth as long as I could.

"You were fantastic. Why didn't you tell me that you would be there?" I said.

"Did you have a good time?" Her face didn't change, but her hand shook.

"Yeah, I did. We had an act, Ethan and me. I was the one in a bear suit. I think people liked it." She didn't say anything, so I kept going. "I loved it. Even though it was different than before."

"That sounds wonderful." She sipped tea. I eased down into a chair, and she smiled at me. "Would you like something to eat?"

"No thanks, I ate at the party. Did you see it?" I asked. "Our act?"

She spoke to the mug in her hands. "I missed it. I'm so sorry, Newt. I thought I was ready to be back there again, but I was wrong. I thought you *weren't* ready, and I was wrong about that too." She looked around the kitchen.

"Why didn't you tell me you would be in the show?"

"Your dad knew, and Gilda, but that's it. I wasn't sure you'd understand. I didn't want you to think I'd forgotten about what happened last year." She squeezed my arm, and her eyes watered. I wanted her to talk about the stage, where I didn't think about the bear at all. I wanted her to tell me if she had the same staticky feelings. She could say if it felt like her heart would come out of her chest too. But she didn't. "I never forget. I worry about you all the time. I know it's not the same as what you went through, but all that worry makes a weight."

I nodded.

"I've been so sad. It's exhausting. I wanted it to feel like it did before, like I could get up there and not worry about anything except what was happening onstage. It wasn't the same, but it was good." She held a finger up. "No. That's not the right word. It's necessary. I thought if it worked, I could get you to try it too. We need healthy escapes. But still, it was hard. I stayed in the truck until it was time to go on, and I left right after. I'm sorry I didn't see your act."

She looked like she wanted me to say something back, that I should tell her it was okay, but I asked, "Is that why you went out on the lake in the swan boat?"

Her head snapped up, and she got a wrinkle between her eyebrows. "When did you see me do that?"

She was full of secrets and sadness. I stared at her. "How often do you go out there?"

She half laughed. "It's what I do when I need a break. Or I need to think. I didn't realize anyone knew."

"And you take the goats? And Chuck?"

"Chuck likes the water. Some of the goats do too. I figured if being on the water made me feel better, maybe it would relax them too." She shrugged, like it was totally normal.

The best thing about being awake and not dreaming is that you can make your own choices. I tried it out in my head three times before I said it out loud.

"It's ok. Maybe you'll see our act next time." It wasn't totally fine, but it would be all right. "Your act, the whole thing . . . it was really wonderful."

Mom kissed my head on her way out of the kitchen. I stood up from my chair, and it almost felt like I was onstage again. My skin buzzed, but this time the feeling stretched over the whole room.

CHAPTER 25

Sunday afternoon, while Mom talked to Carlos on the phone about his new job, I yelled that I was going to the bluff with Ethan.

Today was the Rooster rescue and the last thing I did before we left was lie to my mom.

In the backyard, Ethan and Izzy fed the goats dandelion leaves through the fence. Izzy brought a bike with plastic between the spokes like stained glass and a suitcase mounted behind the seat for a basket.

"It used to be my grandma Gertrude's." She gave it a gentle little pat.

Ethan had his bike too, and his backpack, stuffed to the zipper.

"What's in there?" I said.

"Emergency supplies." He unzipped the top so we could see. "Water bottles, hats, rope, chocolate, a pocketknife, whistles, a box of tissues, and sandwiches." He zipped it back up and tied it to his bike with bungee cords. "Did you guys bring anything?"

"Just the keys," I said. I jumped up and down so they would jingle in my pocket, but quarters flew out into the grass. "And money. Let's go."

I rode on Izzy's handlebars, because I don't trust Ethan, but it felt like she hit every bump in the road. By the time we got to the bike rack on the dock, I knew I'd roped my friends into a terrible idea. It felt like ten years since I'd stood in this spot and hoped for a new bike. I paid our fares with the money Arlene gave me for moving books. Ethan asked the toll taker if the ferry would ever consider accepting Murphy bucks. He frowned and said no.

"I've found six four-leaf clovers, but none on the island. Yet," Izzy said as we boarded the ferry.

"Does that make us unlucky?" I asked.

"It means the odds usually seem better somewhere else," she said.

"Never tell me the odds!" Ethan yelled, like it was a punch line, but we didn't laugh. "What did you do with them?"

"I didn't do anything with them," she said, "but I took pictures. I left them for someone else to see or pick."

"You want them to take the luck?" Ethan asked. I felt the rabbit's foot and the Rooster key in my pocket.

"Taking the clovers isn't going to give me luck." Izzy fiddled with a bracelet made from tiny cockleshells. "Maybe I got some of the luck by finding them. Or maybe I'll get more luck by leaving them there so they can spread, or someone else can get luck too."

"Do you feel any luckier now?" Ethan asked.

"Nope."

"Too bad. We're going to need all the luck we can get today." We sat hip to hip on a chest full of life vests. Izzy pulled the new island brochure out of her back pocket to show me, but I'd already seen a copy at school. I turned to the *W* page for "water bears." Lyric had drawn a pudgy little creature swimming toward algae. I read my entry.

> **WATER BEARS:** *Water bears, or tardigrades, are almost-invisible micro-animals that look like chubby alien bears with eight legs. They eat algae and bacteria. Water bears can survive and adapt to a wide variety of extreme conditions, like subzero ice, boiling water, and being*

launched into outer space. Most go unnoticed,
smaller than a grain of salt, but they can be
found in water around Murphy Island and on
all seven continents.

I got a fist bump.

I wanted to give Ethan and Izzy the choice not to come before we left the dock. I could be brave and go on my own. Huxley was my responsibility, the Rooster was my truck, and it was my problem. I didn't want anything to happen to them.

Ethan read my mind. "Don't even think about it, Fig," he said. "This is the treasure hunt I've been waiting for."

"You don't have to do it." I looked from Ethan to Izzy. "Either of you. Really."

"Sure we do," Izzy said. "You need my four-leaf-clover luck."

"My mom is hosting a silent meditation group all day," Ethan said. "I'm not going home." The ferry left Murphy with a lurch, burping biodiesel fumes across the channel. The island grew smaller. I tried to memorize everything, just in case we never made it back.

"We're going to be okay," Ethan said. He passed me some chocolate.

"What are you talking about?" I broke off a piece and handed the rest to Izzy.

"People usually feel better if they think they know what's going to happen," he said.

Izzy rolled her eyes. "But you *don't* know," she said.

"Maybe I have a theory, and it's right. Then I *do* know."

"That's not the same," Izzy said.

"Agree to disagree," Ethan said.

We flipped through the rest of the brochure, and Ethan added fun facts that people had missed. I told him nobody else cared that much about the history of the harbor, and he laughed like I was kidding. Izzy asked him about Truman Murphy, and his answer lasted the rest of the ferry ride.

We didn't talk much on the walk from the dock to Minerva Antiques & Oddities. Maybe the Rooster wouldn't be there. Maybe I'd made the whole thing up because of the fever. But we found the right address on a run-down brick building three stories tall with vines up the side. Tall glass-and-steel buildings surrounded it, so the store sat in greasy shadows. Steam puffed out of manhole covers down an empty street.

There was no sign, but the Rooster sat right in front, parked between the van we saw on the ferry and a glittery orange lowrider with wooden-bead seat covers. I checked the keys in my pocket for the tenth time.

"All right, let's get it!" Izzy said. They looked relieved, mission accomplished. But my stomach dropped.

"We can't," I said. "It doesn't reverse. We can't move it unless one of the other cars leaves." Ethan groaned.

"What if we pushed it back and forth until you could zigzag out?" Izzy said. There was barely enough room to even stand between the Rooster and the other cars.

I shook my head. "You'd get squished. It wouldn't work." The Rooster was stuck. We didn't have a plan B. I walked down the street toward a car parked partly on the curb and a stray cat asleep under a grocery cart. We'd come all the way here to look at a parked truck. I'd used the money I saved from Arlene for nothing.

It was all for nothing.

"We could wait for Mr. Mustard to come out, and take the truck when he leaves," Izzy offered. It was a good idea, but there was nowhere to hide and keep watch. He'd see us as soon as he came outside.

"Well, that's the end of that," Ethan said. "Can we swing by the coin shop on the way home?"

I listened, but my ears were buzzing like they did onstage. My feet acted before my brain worked, and I walked toward the brick building. It didn't have a sign anywhere, but a window display showed a skeleton in an astronaut's suit, sitting in a big leather chair by a phonograph player. Fuzzy dice like the Rooster's hung off a lamp. The same owl from the truck swung on a rusty hinge over the door next to the window. I pulled the door open and stepped inside. Izzy and Ethan caught up and ducked in before the door closed. My eyes adjusted to the darkness. I wished I had worn a milagro. Or called Carlos. Too late now.

A maze of tall shelves stretched left and right. We waited for someone to come see who'd jingled the bell, but the whole place was still. Ethan stared with wide eyes. I headed down the left aisle, and they followed closely enough that I could hear them breathing. Old typewriters, cameras, and books covered the lower shelves. Dead animals sat frozen on the top. We studied an antelope head mounted on the wall, a stuffed badger, and a coiled rattlesnake in a glass case. It felt like we were trespassing in a museum. The animals watched us with dead marble eyes.

Ethan pointed at a fat bird. "Is that a dodo?"

"What is this place?" Izzy whispered.

We passed a dusty framed box of butterflies and beetles pinned to a board, lit from behind. I leaned in toward a giant green beetle. Ethan's finger got an inch from the beetle's wing before I swatted it away.

"No one is here. Let's go," Ethan said, but twangy music

played from the back of the store. I turned the corner, past a leather trunk that looked like it had come off a pirate ship. I jumped back into Ethan and Izzy. We yelled. A giant owl perched over the trunk like he might swoop down on intruders, but he was as much a goner as everything else in the room. Maybe even us.

We were turning to leave when the floor creaked behind us.

CHAPTER 26

"**What are you** doing here?" Mr. Mustard stood beside a shelf full of old clocks. For once he wasn't wearing the mustard jacket.

"You took my truck. I would like it back," I said. "Please. It was a birthday present from my dad." Ethan and Izzy nodded.

"I'm sorry, son. The truck held something of mine that an associate failed to return to me. Taking the truck was the easiest way for me to bring it back."

"So you stole it?" Ethan said. "That's illegal."

Izzy shushed him, but Mr. Mustard stopped her.

"It's unfortunate that it came to that. But I'm very aware that you haven't been driving the truck legally." He squinted at us and scratched his chin. "You don't possess the title. I have tracked it down and acquired it for a nominal fee. That truck is an eyesore, but it held something very special, as I'm sure you know by now."

For the first time in my life, my spine actually tingled. I shifted my feet and hoped the fidgeting covered my shaking knee. Ethan's eyes darted from shelf to shelf. His fingers fiddled with the lock on the trunk. This was probably his version of heaven.

"Why would someone who sells antiques watch Newt?" Ethan asked.

Mr. Mustard looked at us for a long time before he answered. "I find oddities. I came out to Murphy Island to investigate the sighting of your lake serpent, see if any interesting opportunities arose. Certain parties will pay for clear photographs and other evidence. I couldn't believe my luck when I saw you and recognized the item I had been seeking. Serendipity."

"Okay, but his dad gave him the truck for a birthday present," Ethan said. "He needs it to get around the island. He doesn't even have a bike."

"Unfortunately, it was not your father's to give. It wasn't his fault. The person he won it from had no right to wager it—it was only supposed to be in his possession temporarily." He straightened a javelina with ridiculous teeth on a shelf. "No need to play coy, children. I know that it's not merely the automobile that Mr. Gomez here wants. I believe you have discovered something within the truck with powers beyond your comprehension." Mr. Mustard looked at each of us.

"Can you keep it and let Newt have the truck?" Izzy tilted her head and held her hands out, like the compromise would be a gift. We would be doing him a favor.

"I've already removed my item," Mr. Mustard said. "I no longer want the truck, but it would not be responsible or prudent to return it to unlicensed drivers. Perhaps your father might come to collect it."

If Dad found out that we'd come to Lincoln alone and found the truck, he would flip.

"I don't think so," I said.

"There's one other option," Mr. Mustard said. "I did some research. That kind of truck is a collectible—new restaurants on wheels pop up all the time. Perhaps we could sell it and split the proceeds. I would take my share and send you the remainder."

"Like a . . . valuable collectible?" Ethan smiled. I didn't think my dad would have won anything that valuable in a bet, but Mr. Mustard told us what we could sell it for, and I choked. It was enough to buy new bikes for half the kids on the island. All I wanted was one.

I'd started getting used to the truck, but the best part was Huxley. If Mr. Mustard sold the truck, I could give Izzy and

Ethan some of the money, get a bike, and Mom and Dad could use the rest for supplies to fix the roof, and anything else they needed. Something for Leti too.

"Are you sure you don't want to keep it?" Izzy whispered. "You're getting so good at driving."

"I can wait." Three more years and I could get a driver's license fair and square. If I wanted one.

I handed over the rabbit's-foot key, and Mr. Mustard walked us out to the sidewalk. He promised to send the money as soon as he sold it. I wrote down our address and left Dad's number. It was as fair a deal as we were going to get. I studied the Rooster so I wouldn't forget the details. I was happy to not have to worry about odd jobs and hiding from the sheriff. But I couldn't talk to Huxley anymore or take off when I needed space.

I focused on one step at a time. We turned the corner just as Mr. Mustard whistled. He stood next to the Rooster, the back doors open.

"I believe you forgot something, son," he said. "That bear is quite heavy, and I don't fancy carrying it to the dumpster without a tetanus shot. You have to take it with you."

"What?" We jogged back. Huxley was in the back of the truck. "You want us to take the bear?" I looked at Izzy and Ethan. Mr. Mustard said he took his magical item, but Huxley was still inside. "Isn't that what you've been after? You want Huxley because"—I lowered my voice—"because he grants wishes?"

Mr. Mustard looked at us like we were tiny microbes.

Ethan launched into his story about Boxwood, but Mr. Mustard held up a hand. "The power you describe . . . was perhaps from another source." He glanced toward the store window. "A hidden source. Something tucked away somewhere unexpected. Or maybe it never existed. Fortune comes and goes like a tide."

"It wasn't only good luck," I said. My neck prickled. "I didn't believe it either. Until I did." Mr. Mustard broke eye contact and studied the sidewalk. He crossed his arms.

"Taking the entire truck may have been undue, but I needed time to search away from interference. If you don't have means to carry the statue, I'm afraid it will end up in the dumpster. It's too water damaged to sell, and no one will want to buy a truck with a bear in it."

"We'll definitely take him," I said. "We can use that." I pointed down the street to the abandoned grocery cart on the corner. Ethan ran to get it. I climbed into the truck. Everything looked the same, smelled the same, even creaked the same.

I leaned my forehead on Huxley's and looked into his

green glass eyes. I tried to feel certain about wanting to leave Murphy Island behind, but I wasn't sure of anything. If I had wished right after we found him, I would have missed so much.

I hugged Huxley's barnacle-covered body. I took three deep breaths and whispered the most important wish I could, hopefully loud enough for Huxley but too quiet for anyone else.

"Thanks for letting me get my bear." I looked around the truck. I couldn't figure out what Mr. Mustard had wanted, if not Huxley. Ethan and Izzy climbed in to help me slide Huxley down to the cart before Mr. Mustard changed his mind.

"Where are the fuzzy dice?" Izzy asked. She was right. They weren't on the mirror. I pointed toward the fuzzy dice near the skeleton astronaut in the window. Ethan gasped. Mr. Mustard glanced at the window and smiled.

"So there really was something magical? Like, real magic?" I held my breath.

"The world is full of magic, but not always where our gaze lands. This is goodbye, children. Be well." He said "children" like maybe he wanted to irritate us one last time. It worked. We put Huxley in the cart and headed back down the street. The wheels whined like they'd never had to carry a formerly maybe-magic bear before. We all pushed, Izzy on one side of me and Ethan on the other. Izzy looked back twice.

"He's still watching," she said.

"Let's sneak back and grab that dodo," Ethan whispered, but we shushed him.

"Just keep walking," I said.

We didn't stop until we'd turned two corners. Then we hid behind a tree. Izzy held the shopping cart handle while Ethan climbed over the side and sat down in front of Huxley. We took turns giving each other rides over flat parts and down hills that wouldn't kill us. I almost knocked out my teeth when Ethan hit a curb.

"Switch," Izzy said, and held the cart steady so I could climb out.

"Hang on." I held the street sign for balance while I stretched out my knee.

I knew this street. One way led back to the harbor and the other crossed Carlos's road and led almost right to the street where my grandma lived. We could go straight to abuela's. She would feed us fideo and albóndigas. We could find the raspado man and sit on abuela's porch steps, crunching ice and telling everybody how we'd figured it all out. Carlos could give Ethan and Izzy a ride back to the dock, and I could stay there. I wouldn't ever have to get on the ferry unless I felt like it.

But I wouldn't see Ethan, Izzy, Leti, or my parents. Or Chuck, and Margie and the other goats. There would be no festival next year—at least, not for me. My grandma might not let me keep Huxley. But she would be happy to see me. It would be a new start. I closed my eyes and tried to feel a pull, like a tide, but I had to make the decision myself.

I pushed the cart down the sidewalk, and after a minute Izzy and Ethan followed. My leg hurt, but I wanted to push Huxley myself. The squeaky wheels dragged over the cement like they wanted to turn around, but I knew the way.

CHAPTER 27

The ferry captain said we had to leave the grocery cart in Lincoln.

We stuck Huxley in a safe spot on the starboard deck and celebrated our victory with a heap of candy and sodas from the galley. Ethan opened a pack of gummy bears and plopped on the bench with his feet on his supply bag. Izzy and I stood on either side of Huxley. The ferry pointed toward faraway mountains before it turned the horizon into possibilities.

"That was actually kind of fun." I grinned.

"We should have grabbed that dodo on the way out," Ethan said. "It's got to be worth something, right?" We laughed, but I don't think he was joking. "I can't believe we don't get any more wishes," he said. "You didn't even get to wish." He frowned at the water.

"I'm right where I want to be." I waited for him to look up and nodded. "And I wished today."

"Why didn't you wish the first time I told you? Or as soon as you believed?" A couple gave us a strange look, so I waited until they passed.

"I think deep down I knew that whatever I wanted right then was only going to make part of me happy. I was waiting . . . until I wanted something for the whole me." Nobody said anything. We drank our sodas, ate gummies, and watched the wake stretch back to where we'd already been.

"I almost wished the other day, before it got stolen," Izzy said. "But I wanted to try something else first." A red jellyfish floated by like a lost umbrella from the storm. Izzy played with the zipper on her sweatshirt.

"I didn't know what to wish for before, because there was so much I wanted," I said. "But you having a safe home was bigger than any of my stuff. I wished that you would get to go back to Lincoln and be happy and safe." Izzy stared at me. She could have said, "That's wonderful. Thank you so much for using your wish on me. That's amazing. Thank you."

"You wasted your wish, dummy," she said. "You should have wished for world peace or something."

Ethan glared at me, but I looked at the deck. "I didn't know if that would work. But I wished for things to be better for you, and that's what's happening, right?" I gave Huxley a squeeze when they looked away, even though he wasn't responsible.

"That's not even what I want," she said. "I mean, I want to be happy and safe, but I want to stay on the island. That's what I would have wished for. If my mom can get a job on the island, we'll stay."

"Are you kidding? That's even better!"

"Newt, listen," she said. "Don't get mad."

"Why would I get mad?"

"I've got something else to tell you. I should've said something already. I think Huxley was my great-great-grandma Gertrude's. I didn't recognize it at first, but I checked some photos at the house. I think it's the same bear."

"What?"

"She was a magician, so I guess maybe it could be magic? I don't know. She had that bear act, so maybe someone made it for her. It was on her back deck by the beach my whole life, and now it's not. I should have told you earlier, but I wasn't sure. And then it was making you happy, and I didn't want to take that away."

"Oh! Do you want him back now?" I held my breath.

"Nah, I think he wanted to be out in the world," she said. I almost wished we didn't know where Huxley came from. Either way, he was back now.

"If Huxley was really magic, you could have blown everything and sent me back to Lincoln!" Izzy shrugged. She was totally right. A wish can't change what has already happened.

"You should have told us," Ethan said. "Then maybe Newt would've gotten to wish for something else." Izzy rolled her eyes.

"I didn't waste my wish," I said.

"What are we going to do for the rest of the summer?" Ethan asked. "And what are you going to do with the money?" We had so many possibilities. We rode in peaceful silence, listening to the gulls and the sounds of happy people in the galley.

"You guys. What was in those dice?" Ethan asked.

We looked at each other, but nobody answered. The ferry pushed us farther away from the mainland through invisible currents around the bend, until I could make out the old Murphy Ferris wheel on the horizon. Multicolored houses with mossy roofs lined the harbor and coves like flotsam and jetsam. The clear ringing of the whale bell carried over the water. I scanned the ripples and waves in the ocean around us. It's hard to imagine anything below the surface. It feels flat and unbreakable, like the world ends where the light stops. But it's the top of a cosmos full of fish and alien ocean plants and whales like giants. You can go years on boats without seeing a whale. Other times, if you have perfect luck and your timing is just right, you can catch a back or tail, if not the whole thing. I held my breath and waited.

We all saw it.

CHAPTER 28

Thunder and rain made the squirrels run around the attic all night, but morning brought a show-off blue sky. Each warm, new mishmash piece of me clicked together before I finally got up.

Little Leti came to borrow a book. She wanted the one about the kid reliving the same birthday over and over, but I recommended a couple of ghost stories and the Mars colonization one too. She started reading right there on my floor.

A greasy bag of day-old pan dulce sat on the table in the empty kitchen. Dad sang a Spanish love song in the shower.

I picked up the phone and hung it up again. I ate a galleta first, chewing slowly until the last anise seed disappeared. I brushed my teeth, as if I was about to talk to my grandma in person. I picked up the phone again and called.

"¡Hola, mijo!" she said, like she couldn't imagine anyone she'd rather hear on the phone. "How are you feeling?"

"Good. There's something I want to tell you, abuela." I swallowed and moved around the kitchen. "I think I want to try staying on the island for a while longer. Maybe it's not so bad."

"All right, mi amor. You are always welcome here, no matter what." We talked about her bingo game, and a movie she saw with my tías. She gave up pretty easy, but that's all right, I guess. She's got her own old-lady stuff to do. I went up to take a shower and wash the lump out of my throat.

The next time I came downstairs, Mom was making omelets and Leti was drawing zombies at the kitchen table.

"Where's the truck?" Leti asked. "I want you to give Ramona and me a ride to the spring pool."

"It's gone for good." Leti sighed and slumped in her chair. "I got the bear back, though." Mom nodded like it made sense. "The bear doesn't grant wishes. But he's good luck."

"Can we see him?" Leti asked.

"Sure, and I'll walk you and Ramona to the pool tomorrow if you want," I said, and she almost bounced out of her chair. "We can do some fun stuff this summer while Mom and Dad are at work." Mom winked at me and mouthed "Thank you."

After breakfast, she took Leti outside to help move a tree that had fallen in the storm. Leti wanted to use a chainsaw. Mom said no but let her take some chops with the axe. I crossed my fingers that they would be safe and headed outside to clean the goat pen.

Mom's laugh carried across the garden. I treated the goats to some new hay. As I laid down the last of it, Mom leaned over the fence. Chuck trotted up behind her.

"We're going to make another birthday cake tonight, since your dad missed the last one," she said. "I'll pick up some candles after work."

"I don't need candles," I said, and I meant it. "I'm good for wishes for a while. I'm sorry you never got to make your wish."

"Who says I didn't?" She climbed the fence and sat balanced on the post.

"Did you?" I asked.

She nodded. "Right after you told me about it," she said. "Like, that night after you fell asleep. I twisted my ankle getting out here as quick as I could."

"Did you wish to fly?" I said. "To be a crow?" I pictured her in the festival, warm light shining over her giant inky wings.

"Of course not," she said. She rubbed moss off the fence post. "I wished for you to be happy. For you and Carlos and

Leti to have a good life. That's all I ever wish for. For you all to be brave and fierce and happy."

"What?" I stood up and really looked at her. She said she would wish to fly. Some days I wasn't sure if she even saw us.

"Shooting stars, birthday candles, dandelion puffs. You get them all, mijo. You are a survivor. And you are our ancestors' wildest dreams. We can't wait to see what you do."

A butterfly landed on my shoulder, and I stayed as still as I could so I wouldn't scare it. We watched its wings fold open.

"Thanks, Mom." She scratched Greta behind the horns, and I rubbed Porridge's belly. I cleared my throat. "You know, I'm thinking about staying on the island. But I still want to go to Lincoln Bay next year. If that's still okay."

"It's more than okay." She beamed. "You're growing up into a pretty great guy. The island needs you. The mainland can wait." We laughed, and the goats bleated. They like to feel in on the conversation.

"What were you going to do with Leti all summer if I was in Lincoln?" I asked. "Who would watch her while you were working?"

"We would've figured it out. She's starting to get old enough to stay home a little too. She can try spreading her wings." She patted Greta. "Maybe my wish worked, eh? Your dreams are gone."

They were, but I didn't want to jinx it. I hadn't woken up from an attack dream since the storm. It wasn't perfect. Sometimes I got shaky and sweaty before I even realized that a memory from that day had bubbled in my brain. I wrote in an old notebook a lot. Writing made it better. Something like that takes more than wishing.

We watched the butterfly rise up and soar over an invisible swell of air until it became another part of the great, wide sky.

I put some sandwiches and peaches in a bag with a towel and an old pair of Carlos's swim trunks, since mine don't fit anymore.

Chuck saw a squirrel eating oxalis and pulled the leash so hard it almost yanked my arm out of the socket. I wished I still had the Rooster, but the exercise was good for my leg, I guess. Ethan came by with some licorice and Boxwood. We walked to the beach to see what the tide had washed up. The whole island smelled like a new start.

"Ethan, listen. I'm staying on the island, but I'm still going to try out Lincoln Bay next year. They have a lot of cool stuff, and I'll get to spend more time with my dad's side of the family."

"But you'll live on the island?"

"I'll live on the island," I said.

Ethan smiled. "You're gonna miss seeing me in class. Eating lunch in the pool. Volunteering at the museum . . ." He trailed off, and I shrugged.

"Maybe," I said. He bumped my shoulder, and I laughed. "I definitely will, but we can still hang out, and do our homework together, and go to the beach!" I pointed at the whirligigs over us marking the path across the island.

We passed Dad and Leti by the lake. He's been spending less time there since the big storm, but they sat on a bench sharing a bag of popcorn from Herb's, like they expected Marvelo to turn up and put on a show any minute. I yelled hello, and they waved like they hadn't seen me in days.

"You'll be home in time to rehearse for the festival if you catch the early ferry," Ethan said.

"We'll see." We already had a secret plan for what to do next year.

Ethan kept looking at me funny, but he would look away when I looked back. We passed the notice board at Herb's. Flyers for a new kids' basketball league and a free bike hung over my faded found-bear-statue flyer. I tore my old paper down and wrote down the number for the free bike. The seat came from a tractor or something, but I could switch it for something better. I wrote down the number for the basketball club too, for Leti.

Ethan looked at me. "I thought you'd get a new bike with

the Rooster money," he said. Dad had offered to take me bike shopping when we got paid, but it didn't seem like such a big deal anymore. Ethan sighed.

"What?" I asked.

"Nothing."

"You don't want me to get the bike?"

"The bike is fine," he said. I waited. He walked away with his head down.

"At least we'll be ready if we ever find something that grants wishes again," I said. Our odds are probably better of finding a whole mastodon on top of a pile of old coins, but you never know.

We let Chuck and Boxwood off their leashes, and they chased swallows they could never catch. We zigzagged down the beach to the pier to visit Huxley. The beach is different now. You'd only notice if you spent a lot of time here. Sand and logs had shifted, and the bluff was steeper. Huxley stood where we had left him, close to the beach but far enough from the highest tides. He looks like he's guarding the island, green eyes watching the sea. Izzy thinks maybe his wishbone is a slingshot after all. Izzy's mom said he could live on the beach instead of in their backyard. He is special, even if he doesn't grant wishes. If anybody wants to come talk to him, they can. He was too heavy to carry across the island anyway.

We poked around in the tide line and found a wavy rock

that Ethan said could be a fern fossil. I munched on glass-wort and made sure gulls didn't swipe our sandwiches. Ethan looked at me funny again.

"Spit it out already!" I said. I thought he would walk away, but he moved closer.

"I saw it, Newt. I saw Marvelo." His breath smelled like licorice. "Last night. I walked to the lake while I waited for a pizza my mom ordered. I wasn't there two minutes, and I saw it. Thirty feet from shore, the water swelled . . . and there it was. It wasn't a fish, or a log, or anything. It was big. A huge, scaly back. It lasted a few seconds, I don't know how long, and then it was gone." He was breathing hard, like he'd been holding his breath until he told me. "I wanted to tell you so that, you know, you'd know that your dad was telling the truth. Or he could've been. It's there. I promise." Ethan is the first guy I would think of after my dad that might lie about Marvelo. But he looked earnest, and it felt true.

"Are you going to tell anyone?"

"I just did," he said.

"No, I mean . . . for the reward?"

He raked lines in the sand with his fingers, and a wave smoothed them out.

"Nah. If we keep talking about it, sooner or later someone will believe us, and where does that get him? Things would change, and I like the island how it is. I don't have any proof anyway. But . . . it was pretty amazing. Something's there."

He smiled and I smiled, and we poked around in the kelp.

There was nothing to say back.

Ethan held out a tarnished ring. Its stone had fallen out, but you could still see the vine design around the band. Maybe an island visitor lost it a hundred years ago during a masquerade party. Ethan popped the ring into his pocket. Chuck spotted Izzy before we did and lunged down the beach. She was playing in the surf with her mom, splashing and diving in the waves. Boxwood ran after Chuck, and Ethan followed Boxwood. Their crooked, twisting tracks scarred the wet sand before the tide smoothed everything over again.

I ran until my lungs hurt, which didn't take long. But the more I run, the more my leg stretches and feels stronger. I can't erase the attack, but I am getting better at deciding when to think about it. I focused on the warmth of the sun, Izzy's laugh, that good low-tide smell, and Ethan's cartwheels into the ocean swells. I could carry them all with me like invisible milagros.

The light caught inside a tide pool by my foot. A purple crab hid in rubbery kelp beside a bouquet of anemones. I swirled the water around until little specks twinkled in the slosh above the urchins. They could be tiny bits of algae, sand, or Ethan's lost gold dust. But I hoped they were tardigrades— water bears finding their way through the world.

I waved my friends over, and we all looked closer.

ACKNOWLEDGMENTS

Stories need people like tardigrades need water. Here's what I'm thankful for: teachers supporting students in finding what they love about the world; librarians guiding us toward narratives that make us want to raise our own voices; writers and artists speaking their truths and showing it can be done; and publishing professionals getting new stories to readers.

I want to thank friends who offered encouragement and critique. You know who you are. I get lots of vaudeville fun and inspiration volunteering with Seattle's Moisture Festival, the largest comedy/varieté festival in the world. And my life would be very different if I hadn't found the Society of Children's Book Writers and Illustrators and its people. Creative communities are everything.

I love talking with young writers about crafting stories. Thank you for your enthusiasm and courage.

Thank you to Luisa Uribe for creating this dreamy cover and Michelle Cunningham for her superb art direction. I'd also like to thank Barbara Jamison from the Puget Sound Goat Rescue for answering my questions about goats, Dr. Rich Manzi for consulting on the accuracy of Newt's injuries, and Ariela Rudy Zaltman and Polo Orozco for working with us on authentic cultural representation. Any mistakes are my own.

I am so inspired by the team at Pippin Properties for taking care of business with so much heart. I am especially thankful for my beloved agent, Sara Crowe, for her patience and encouragement. Sara, your faith pushed me to finish this story.

Thank you to my editor, Dana Carey, for believing in Newt and helping me to look closer to find the shape of his story. It takes a lot of people to make a book. I appreciate the work and expertise of Wendy Lamb, Tamar Schwartz, Colleen Fellingham, Candice Gianetti, and the rest of the team at Random House Children's Books. Publishing this story is a wish come true.

Thanks to my family. It is not always easy to choose patience, love, and kindness, but you do.

And let's all be grateful for reminders that even on dark days, the world is full of good and wonder down to its weirdest, tiniest parts. Thank you.

ABOUT THE AUTHOR

Kim Baker's first book, *Pickle,* about a secret middle-school prank society, has been selected for many reading lists and was a finalist for the CBC Children's Choice Book of the Year and the Texas Bluebonnet Award. When she was thirteen, she lived above an old movie theater and drove herself to work in a rusty VW van. She now lives in Seattle near panaderías and tide pools but usually far from bears.

kimbakerbooks.com

@kim_bak